Machinist of Mana

★ BOOK 3 ★

MACHINIST OF MANA

BOOK 3

WANDERING AGENT

Podium

Cover design by Yanhong Lu

ISBN: 979-8-89539-877-7

Published in 2026 by Podium Publishing
www.podiumentertainment.com

Podium

MACHINIST OF MANA

✶ BOOK 3 ✶

CHAPTER 1

✶

AGGRAVATING INSTRUCTOR

"I'd like to take you where we need you immediately, kid, but there are some things you need to learn first," the minister said as we met in the small home he'd been assigned.

"What kinds of things?"

"Language, for example. See, there are a few different dialects of the elven language, and while most are . . . at least mostly comprehensible between one another, you need to learn what we call the southern dialect," he explained.

"Never even heard of it, but I think the school offers Atali?"

"Not surprising, as Atali is most similar to the language used in the cores, and the southern dialect is a bit niche, but regardless, that's fine. I'll teach you."

"You?" I asked with a raised eyebrow.

"Nobody better," he replied. "You're supposed to be going in as part of an exchange so that young men and women can see the 'greatness of elven culture,' according to the pamphlets. You see, while our enemy doesn't particularly like humans—rather hates them—they really want to show off. The fact that you're part elf makes it even better, and we'll play that up a bit, make you look more elven than you actually are."

"You can . . . Wait, I have so many questions. First of all, you speak their language well enough to teach it?"

"I speak all of the elven languages, kid, and a few that aren't even spoken anymore. I'm old, older than you would believe, even if I told you, and you won't be the first person I've taught."

"In that case, isn't this a vast waste of your time?"

"Yes and no," he replied, candidly. "Yes in that I'm massively overqualified, but no in that I want to do it, so I'm doing it."

The man before me was one of the several councilors who ruled a city on Elazia. The irritating man had outright refused to tell me his name, simply asking me to refer to him by his title, or by Ambassador, as most of the people here did. I knew almost nothing about him, save that he was powerful, old, and really a giant pain in the neck.

The king, who was still rather displeased with me, had personally green-lit this operation after some discussion with the elf. I suspected it was as much punishment as it was a mission to aid a longtime ally. School would be canceled for me; though there wasn't much I was learning there, anyway. Instead, I would be joining a sort of diplomatic program for the next few months.

Of note, my school was taking an extended break, anyway. It hadn't been attacked, but with the destruction in the city, there was too much going on in the area for the school to run properly. Instead, they were rerouting students here and there, and I was being sent across the world.

"Why do you want to do it, though?" I asked.

"I knew Alana," the councilor said. "I've known several people with that same aura as you, kid."

"I'm not a kid."

"You'll be a kid to me for another century, and don't interrupt. It's childish." My eye twitched. "Right, anyway, you lot never fail to be interesting. Also, the boss wants this done right."

"Another question—who is this boss of yours?"

"You'll meet him again soon enough."

"Again?"

He just smiled in response and pulled out a large book. "Ready to learn, kid?"

The next several hours were intense, but I had to admit, he was good. There were no charts, but there were plenty of tricks he shared with me. I wouldn't be fluent in the near future, but I was learning quickly, getting my head filled to the brim with important bits of grammar and words that I could use immediately.

"This is actually not as bad as I thought," I said as we finished for the day.

"Look, our goal here is to get you through the basics. About a thousand words make up most of any given language, then you just need to fill in the gaps for context. The alphabet is easy, so we can just drill it, and you already know some of it from your studies on the core and whatnot."

Whatnot was English, as there were several turns of phrase and important words that were clearly loan words. Did this man know about me being from another world? I didn't know, and it didn't matter much, as he was assigned as my instructor for the next week or so. My oddly good memory was helping, too, ensuring I learned faster and better than I ever had as a human.

I wondered how much he knew exactly. He knew about the auras. He knew about me knowing odd things; he'd even commented on it. Did this man, or elf, or whatever—I was calling him a man in my head—come from Earth, too? There wasn't exactly a subtle way to ask, and if I was wrong, who knew the consequences. Putting it aside for now, I just worked.

"You'll need a few weeks, at least, to get conversational, but that's fine. We'll take a boat," the councilor declared after a time.

"To the other continent? Why?" I asked.

"Few reasons, really. First, you need the time."

"Okay."

"I also want to check out some things. There have been rumors recently about some odd activities in the sea that I want to check for myself."

"Makes sense, but making this whole thing take longer than it should doesn't really help, does it?"

"Well there's also the last reason, and it's one of the more important ones: I do not want you associated with me."

"Rude."

"You don't want it either, kid. These people you're going to, they're enemies of mine and of others as well. If you are found to be too close to us, it'll cause problems. Going the long way sort of shows that you're not associated. Make sense?"

"Why should I help you against your enemies though? I'm still unclear on that."

"Your ruler trusts me," he said. "Isn't that enough?"

"No," I said, not even blinking.

"I think they killed your old auntie, then. How's that?"

"That would be an act of war, and she died of old age."

"Not old age alone, kid, and it certainly would, but why? Also, my boss is none too pleased about little Alana dying; though he wants proof before he does anything about it."

"Do I get to meet this boss of yours?" I asked.

"Maybe . . . maybe, maybe, maybe," he chimed with a crooked smile.

CHAPTER 2

✶

COMPARING PICTURES

I had a terrific day off from my torturous tutoring, so of course, I was spending part of it helping another study.

"I do hate history class," Rowenna grumbled. "Our teacher is so terribly boring."

"Fair," I admitted with a smile, happy just to spend time with someone else.

"And I feel like I'm falling behind, too, never caught up."

"It is difficult to catch up on history. They're always making more of it."

That comment got my irritated girlfriend to toss one of her books at me, something I slapped away absently.

"Worse with all my cousins here, and their staff. The house is always bustling now. Sure, I love them, but it's all a little much."

Rowenna's house had somehow come out of the attack on the city completely unscathed, one of several such places. They hadn't been targeted, and with enough nobles around, and their people, they'd repelled the few goblins that had come their way handily.

Many, many others weren't so lucky, and while the duke was doing all he could to help, there were places still full to the brim. Every boarding house was full, with families that had the ability to house their kin. It meant that people were practically tripping over each other everywhere they went.

Yet, Rowenna had still managed to secure us some time in her room; though there was, of course, a chaperone.

"Don't throw things! It's unseemly," her auntie griped from a corner. It was the same aunt who'd gotten me to come to her party. "Perhaps it's time for a break, if you're so bothered. We could have some tea and chat for a while . . ." The woman really was a terrible gossip.

"Now, now, ma'am, we're here to make sure Rowenna has no problems with her classes, not to socialize. Mixing the two will cause this whole session to fail," I said with a kind smile, determined to sidestep further attempts at getting me to tell stories about what I'd been doing during the attack. Rumors already abounded. Of course, I didn't inform the woman that I would be leaving for an unknown quantity of time soon, but I was tired of her pressuring me. Letting her wait would be fine.

"Pah, when will I need to know ancient history anyway," Rowenna complained.

About an hour later, her aunt left us to go deal with some business for a moment, and Rowenna sighed.

"You haven't told me much about what you're up to these days," she said as she put her books away.

"I cannot, Rowenna, not because of anything you did, but because of my work. Certainly you understand that?"

"Well, yes, but that doesn't mean I enjoy it. I suppose with your propensity for weapons, much of your personal business is with the military, so it's something I should get used to."

"I imagine your aunt's been insufferable about it," I snickered.

"She has, but if I don't know, I don't know. She probably thinks she'll get answers hovering over us like she is." Rowenna picked up the book she'd tossed, eyes settling on the page it was turned to intensely.

"Something wrong?" I asked.

"No, just, really familiar . . ."

I leaned over, looking at the page and had the same sense. There was something pricking at my brain, just on the corner, but I couldn't piece it together. The face. I knew the face depicted, clearly a copy of some old painting or some such, but from where? Had I seen it around town somewhere? If so, I couldn't place it.

"It's . . ." Suddenly, the girl jumped up, running over to her closet and pulling the doors open, where she found another bound volume, this one with oddly thick pages.

Rowenna brought it to the table and began flipping through the pages rapidly. On each page was a letter I'd sent her over the years, each one pressed into a frame.

"You framed them all?" I asked, surprised.

"Don't tell me you threw out my letters?" she said, sending me a sharp glare.

"No, but I didn't keep them so nicely organized . . ." They were sitting in a bunch in one of my trunks, or at least most of them were . . .

"Something we shall address later, but for now, here it is!" One of the more recent pages was the one she was looking for, and I saw it, the same face that was in her book—the same eyes and jaw. The ears were different, though, but just slightly.

"Oh, I remember now, the man from the town!" I said, slapping myself. "But wait, how is that possible?"

I looked down at her book and read the caption.

DEPICTION OF THE ELVEN KING

My eyes bulged. The image was well over five thousand years old, or at least the original was. The picture in this tome was a reproduction from some palace on the other side of the world. Even his clothes looked like what I'd seen him in—flowing robes and tired eyes, but the eyes in the ancient picture held a fire I couldn't quite match with the man I'd met.

Not that it would have even been possible. Given everything I knew, there'd only ever been one person to call himself a king among the elves. Others had tried to claim the title but were all considered pretenders, their mysterious deaths not long after they'd crowned themselves evidence enough. Theories abounded as to why, but my guess was that someone powerful took offense.

"That's not possible," I muttered. "He'd have to be . . . millennia old."

"Lots of people claim it's nonsense, but they say the purest blooded elves don't age."

"And you believe that?" I asked.

"Well, I think I'm starting to."

"Maybe I should as well," I mumbled. "I don't suppose you'd loan me this book?"

Rowenna's eyes sparkled with mischief. "Go ahead, but you owe me."

"I shudder to imagine what sort of debts I might be incurring."

CHAPTER 3

CONFRONTATION

"How old are you!" I asked my irksome teacher.

"Old enough," he replied without even looking up.

"Like five or six thousand years?"

"Something like that. Honestly, for some of it I didn't count." The elf didn't even look up from the book he was perusing as he spoke to me, seeming not the slightest bit surprised that I'd come to see him, nor worried that I was unhappy. Then again, did he need to be worried?

"Can you take this seriously?" I said, frustrated.

In a moment the world shifted, like someone had pulled the curtain. Outside nothing changed, but as he looked up, as our eyes met, my whole body trembled, not because of some spell, nor some magic he was forcing out. I felt like an ant standing before an elephant, the beast raising its foot to crush me.

"Are you entirely sure that's what you want?" he asked smoothly, eyes still locked on mine.

"What . . . what is?" I stumbled, and the pressure was gone.

"Those like you who use physical magic cannot see it like we can, but that is the power of my aura. Normally, you wouldn't even feel it, but I was practicing magic before humans had the wheel. In other words, *show some respect*."

"Is this the real you, then? An old monster sitting atop his throne?"

"Haha, no. I dislike being like that, but disliking something and being good at it are two different things, and I've had to crush more than my share of enemies."

"Why me?"

"Didn't I already answer this? You're interesting."

"Like him?" I asked, producing Rowenna's book for him, the page marked.

The ambassador flipped it open and smiled, but didn't answer.

"You aren't the boss, kid. Now, are you ready for today's lesson?"

"I've got a lot more questions."

"I'm sure."

"I met him, in a park a while back."

"I know."

"He didn't help stop that monster attacking those kids," I grumbled.

"And you had it well in hand, didn't you? Took care of the beast well enough."

"He said something about his daughter . . ."

"Drop it." Once more his voice took on a cold tone.

"What?"

"Don't bring that up again. There are things that are frankly too prickly, and while I feel I've been very accommodating, there are limits."

We looked over the desk at one another, and I blinked. He could turn me to paste if he wanted to, and we both knew it, but he didn't want to. Moreover, I could tell that it hadn't been a joke or a lie. Something had happened, something that still bothered him, something that caused this man pain. Even more than that, though, it felt more like old personal matters, like prying into someone's family.

"Our lesson then?" I said. "Don't suppose there's a word in the elven language family for 'goblin' or something."

"Interestingly, there is, though it's not used much. The same as in your own language." The same as in English, then, a loan word someone used.

"Wait, how long have the elves known about them, then?" I inquired.

"There are some stories, bedtime stories for children and the like really, that mention them. As for the current strain, they're fairly unknown, or were until recently." What did "recently" even mean to this man, I wondered.

"So, the island they came from?"

"There are a lot of islands in the ocean that aren't well mapped, I'm sad to say. You see, parts of the sea, particularly more southern ones, get really nasty when you get out on the water. Like monsters-the-size-of-palaces nasty."

"Good to know."

"It is, since we'll be taking a boat through some of those waters. Don't worry though. They don't really mess with boats often."

He began to address me in the dialect I was going to need to learn. Our lesson had begun. It irked me how good he was at teaching, particularly when he didn't want to teach me the things I wanted to know. Still, though, we spent a better part of the day getting deeper and deeper into grammar and vocabulary. Personally, even after so little learning, I felt like I could probably stumble through surviving where he was sending me.

At the end of the day, I was exhausted. I'd not even been scheduled for that long of a lesson today, but we'd gone on and on. When I left,

I began thinking on all that I'd learned, for I'd gotten so many hints. This man's 'boss,' whom he'd brought up before my own ruler was the elven king everyone believed dead. The councilor probably knew I was from another world; though, if he did, he was letting it rest. Honestly, I doubted I could provide him with information he didn't already have, though, so why would it even matter to him?

In my previous life, I'd been a fairly humble man, cleverer than many, perhaps, but no genius, no master inventor. My knowledge here was valuable, enough to propel me to make things nobody had seen and approaching them in ways they didn't understand. I'd done my reading, though, and if even half of what was said about the old elven kingdom was true, they'd had more technological advancements than I could make in a lifetime. I suppose with immortality they could just build, up and up, their leader telling them where to go, the paradigms to follow.

Me, though? I was just one man, one more piece on a board bigger than I'd ever known existed. My question was, who all was playing? And what were the stakes?

CHAPTER 4

✶

HEADACHE

"You look depressed, my boy," Grandpa said to me as we lounged around after dinner.

"Just thinking."

"Always important but a dangerous pastime, I find. Whatever has you so bothered?"

"I've done a lot, seen a lot, but I'm not sure that it really changes much."

"What about those nice goblin girls? You certainly changed things for them," he said.

"Yes, but . . ."

"And all the people on that train—what about them?"

"Well, I suppose I did . . ."

"The girl in the tunnel, the children attacked by that monster. Oh, I'm sure I'm forgetting one or two somewhere. Mind helping?"

"That's not really the point, Grandpa," I grumbled.

"It is though. You're doing quite a bit. Those people may seem like nothing compared to some of the people you're rubbing shoulders with now, but they're still important, still worth your effort."

"What made you bring up the people I'm rubbing shoulders with now?" I asked.

"Because I'm no child, Percival, and I've seen my share of things. I've even felt the way you do now. Seen others outpace me, outdo me. It is something we all deal with at times."

"And how does it make you feel?" I asked, trying to put my own feelings into words.

"Proud, mostly, and happy that I get to be part of it all."

It didn't take a genius to realize exactly who he was talking about, which was good for me, since I wasn't one of them. Though his words did still stir my emotions deeply, and I took a few moments to bring them back under control. After that, it wouldn't do at all to lose control of myself here and now.

"I don't suppose you've any advice?" I asked after a few moments spent schooling myself.

"Of course I do, but maybe not on what you were expecting."

"Oh?"

"This man you've been studying with, you need to be careful."

"You think he means me ill?"

"No, if he meant you ill, you'd be dead. I've never met an Ancient before, but I've heard plenty of stories, and if even a fraction of them are true . . . Well, we at least know he doesn't mean you ill. That doesn't mean that whatever you're doing will be good for you though. Think of it like the king did about those passengers on that train. People who are leaders, or others who have power can and will sacrifice those they need to, to achieve their goals. Even if you're doing what you're told, you can still be discarded for advantage, so don't trust what you don't need to, take what advantages you can get, but be ready to abandon whatever tasks your given if you find yourself in danger."

"That's fairly obvious, isn't it?" I said.

"You'd be surprised how often people forget the fairly obvious, Percival. There are no small amount of writings to fully state obvious, stupid things people already know but won't listen to."

That was rather deep, in a way. He was right, too, even thinking back about my experiences from Earth. Sun Tzu, for example, wrote a lot of things that brought on the "Well, duh," reaction, but so many people did them anyway that it seemed a good idea to write them down somewhere. It wasn't any different on this world either.

"A good point. I don't suppose I could impose upon you to continue spreading planes while I'm away?"

"It won't be much of an imposition, Percival. The military stopping me might be the only issue."

I snickered. While the king might not have been pleased with my actions, they had struck a lot of people like a brick to the face. Any fool could see the application of what we'd done and other potential ones. Sure, there were some mages who could fly and wouldn't need our help to engage in those applications, but bringing it to the masses, or at least more people than we currently had, was a major change.

"And keep an eye on Mother for me."

He sighed. "That is harder. Your mother is still processing it all, and while she's tough, it will take time. Honestly, I'm not sure if having you here helps or hurts, but don't get hurt, son. That would crush her."

"She didn't seem bad," I observed.

"It's a brave face for you and others. Your grandma's been spending a lot of time with her, you know, and . . . well, she's still worried."

"Perhaps I should spend more time with her, and sister, too, for that matter."

"That one you'll need to speak with, indeed. Particularly with how much time she's been spending with that goblin priestess." My mind briefly glitched at his comment.

"Wait, what?"

"Were you not told of this?"

"No, I most certainly was not! Why in the world are they spending so much time together?"

"You'll need to speak to your paternal grandparents, if you want more details on that, but I gather they're having rather deep conversations about moral ethics or something."

"Is . . . is that a joke? Why would they . . ." I had a headache just thinking about it.

Sasha had been released from custody some time ago, or mostly released. She was still being monitored, as were all the goblins who came to the surface, the few that there were. We also knew they still had at least some of their kind hidden, and the government wasn't outright ripping up the streets to get at them, yet, but they were definitely watching. It was also known that some of the goblins had escaped into the countryside, rather than fall back to their old home beneath the city, something which I had no doubt would prove to be a thorn in this island's side for, potentially, generations to come.

"Well, looks like you've got at least one more task now," Grandpa said, laughing.

CHAPTER 5

✶

UNLIKELY FRIENDS

I followed through with what I'd learned and set up a slew of meetings. The first of which was with my younger half-sibling. Okay, "set up" was a bit of an exaggeration. It's more like I showed up at our grandparents' house unannounced, and I was quite glad I did.

"You know I'd heard about this, but I didn't quite believe it," I said as I looked at the two girls sitting and sipping tea, one pale, the other green.

"There's no need to sound accusatory," my sister said, keeping her face straight. I was happy that she was no longer referring to me as Lord Percival, but it seemed she was putting on a show for her friend.

"Surprised, that either of you are doing this." I looked at the other member of this tea party.

"One of the local men, Ignus, believed it best we try to meet a few people. If you have an issue with us meeting, you might take it up with him."

"I'll certainly do that, but why her?" I asked Sasha.

"I'm right here, you know."

Sasha offered a calming smile to Kaylee before continuing. "Because she was the only person who looked nearly as out of sort as me. Believe it or not, I don't know a lot of humans, other than you, and you're not exactly friendly."

"A fair point."

"But Kaylee looked so out of place that it resonated with me. I understood it. Since I was in the palace, and wanted to meet someone anyway to build bridges, we talked."

"This is a massive headache. We need to get Kaylee into a few introductory parties soon, and I know people will ask about you when they meet her. If I know, others do too."

"That's not a problem."

"It is, because they'll want you to come, basically as a form of entertainment, like something in a zoo they can look at. That will get you meeting more people, but not in a good way."

"Do you think I don't understand that already? I do, and even if they don't respect me at the beginning, they still need to see that not all of us are like the ones who destroyed so many people's homes."

She had a point. Perhaps I was being overly protective of Kaylee, and a bit condescending to Sasha, but this situation still rankled.

"I'm sitting right here too. You can't just cut me out of this," Kaylee interjected, looking none too pleased. "I'm not just someone you can tell what to do and ignore."

That stung.

"You're right, Kaylee, but please listen. Things are going to be hard already. You're already a scandal on your own. Adding Sasha to the mix will only cause rumors to fly like never before."

"Do you think I don't know that? Perhaps I'm not a mechanical genius Lor—Percival, but I'm not a fool." I heard her stumble and sighed.

"I know you're not, but this isn't a world you know yet. Do you think I can do anything immediately? No, I can't. I have to ease my way into it. Kaylee, I won't be here for much longer, and I worry for you."

"Others do too, Brother."

"At the very least, try talking to Rowenna a bit. She's about your age and has a good grip on things. She'll be able to help you more than I will, in all likelihood, so long as you don't irritate her."

"She did send me a letter the other day . . ."

"And you responded promptly, right?"

"Um . . ."

I frowned and looked for a paper to roll up and smack her on the head with. Sadly, there were none at this particular tea party, so I had to make do with clear exasperation.

"You need to do so immediately, and apologize in the letter. It's considered proper form to answer as soon as possible, which you should know. I'd ask Grandmother to look it over before you send it too. Kaylee you have few resources that you can bring to bear just now, and you really need to use them as well as you can."

Of course I'd be going to see her, too, and apologize myself. Really, Kaylee needed friends her own age and in her new social group, and there were few candidates better suited to the task than my girlfriend. Having them at odds would cause me no end of trouble, but I didn't think my sister had meant to offend.

Tired of arguing, I flopped down, absolutely lacking the style I normally tried to put forth. Fooling Kaylee seemed stupid, and I very much doubted the goblin girl, who'd lived in the sewers her whole life, cared a lick. This was one of the few times that I could actually just relax and do anything.

"My mother is . . . I'm worried about her, and while I know you probably have no desire to see her, or her you, I'd appreciate it if you kept in contact with someone she might, someone who can keep an eye on her," I said as I filled a cup of tea for myself.

"Is there anything we can do?" asked Kaylee.

"Probably not, but I'd like you to keep an ear to the ground, regardless." Taking a deep drink of the scalding leaf water, I continued. "Grandpa is keeping an ear out, too, of course, but he's not a woman. He sees things from a very different perspective."

"I seriously doubt that will change things much," Sasha said.

"It does, not because of some innate thing, but because of social ones. People respond differently, act differently, and are shown different sides. You should learn that if you ever want to integrate yourself into human society." I made a face at my cup. "This badly needs sugar."

"Do you have anything else you'd like to say, perhaps something to suggest other than just critiquing my tea?"

"No, but I might have an idea. Something to get you out in the world and make a big enough splash that it won't be too obvious." It had hit me as I was looking into the cup. A plan. If I could get everyone on board, at least.

CHAPTER 6

★

INTRODUCTION PLAN

"I can't believe you agreed to this," I said.

"I can't believe you thought I wouldn't. Do you even know the last time I went to a human party? It's been so long, so incredibly long since I did something like this, and I know it'll be fun. Adding your new friend is going to be the best thing I've seen in decades." The ambassador chuckled, mischief in his voice.

"Aren't you worried about people seeing you here, knowing you're doing this?" I asked.

"Oh, the ones who matter don't know I'm here," he said with a dismissive wave. "They'll think I'm one of the other councilors. If someone who mattered actually saw me, it might be an issue, but I've already vetted the people at your little soiree, and the staff."

"What? How?" I asked, surprised.

"Long years of practice." I'd learned over the last few weeks that that meant he wasn't going to tell me. So, I decided to quote a bit of fiction from my previous world.

"All right then, keep your secrets." It seemed an appropriate thing to say to an ancient magus who was often a pain in the neck.

"You say that as if it were ever in question?"

With a sigh I continued. "And it's not my party; it's Rowenna's."

Now that had taken almost no doing at all. I was sure her aunt would have loved to host this one, but I didn't particularly love the woman, so I'd asked Rowenna to take care of it instead. She had two non-humans of note attending her event, something almost nobody ever did. Plus, this was the first public appearance of one species, save their violent introductions to ours. Basically, this was going to be the event of the year, a year in which nothing was going on in the city other than repairs.

"I am also more than familiar with making others take credit for your actions."

"Can we focus on brighter things?"

"Like the evening's events? Why, certainly! I have nothing of note to do here, but since my young friend, a hero from the nation's capital, invited me to join him for the night, I will admit, I was honored. Similarly, it is a rare chance for me to mingle with your people, and do what I'm here to do, ambass."

"I don't think *ambass* is a word," I pointed out.

"Which of us is the ambassador?"

"Um . . ."

"Then I shall decide, shouldn't I? After all, who'd know better than me?"

"Could you be normal? Just for tonight?"

"Sure, I'll act all uptight for you, but know that I'll be laughing on the inside. On a brighter note . . ." He looked across the small waiting room we were in at the other guest of honor. "It's a pleasure to meet you."

The goblin priestess had chosen, or been led to choose, a conservative number. It was similar in cut, though distinctly different in some other ways, to the normal work clothes of the Order. The fabric was higher quality, with decorations and embellishments, but it still looked like something a priest might wear to an event like this one. That was good. It would, on some level, reinforce what we were trying to get people to think of her and her people—as just other people. People who'd been misled into attacking us, people whose bad elements had been quashed.

"Um . . . you as well," Sasha faltered, reaching out to take the man's hand. "I'm Sasha, sir, leader of the goblins here in Exion."

"Glad to hear you got that settled."

"There really was nobody else. My sister wouldn't touch the position with an extended pole, and most of the rest of our siblings are dead or fleeing."

Fleeing was a problem, but not mine, and not today. There were already calls for us to be rid of the goblins we had, like they had somewhere to go. That would fall to others though. For now we just needed to get through this party.

Kaylee and Rowenna joined us shortly thereafter, the former looking exhausted and the latter looking almost satisfied.

"The guests will arrive soon," Rowenna declared.

And they did. For most of the night, Kaylee stayed near either me or Rowenna, letting us make introductions to people she didn't know. That in itself was a help, but the bigger one was that everyone was distracted by the shiny new toys in our midst. Toys they didn't want to lose access to because they'd offended a family member of the host's boyfriend.

Kaylee did fine. She was clearly nervous, a bit withdrawn and shy, but that was all normal. Most girls who were new to public events were like that—a bit shaky on what to do, like newborn deer taking their first steps into a world they didn't know. While most families made sure to fix that by going to events all the time, there were always a few new people in the city every year who'd come from far-flung families, relatives that lived too far out in the middle of nowhere to have had much experience.

No, the real issue was my teacher who, despite his earlier words, still gave off waves of rakishness. He saw every barb thrown around and responded in kind, words expertly crafted to shut people down when he wanted.

"I'm glad to see at least *you're* civilized. There have been so many worries of late. It's good to see a leader that will listen to others," a woman said to Sasha, dripping insult. The poor girl was clearly getting that, but not quite sure what to do about it.

"Ah, listening to others is indeed important," my elven instructor chimed in. "You see, too often those without proper experience try to lead those whose advice they should rather heed. Why, the stories I could tell you of people who made such mistakes. I see them again and again, fools jumped up upon their own belief in their superiority. It's embarrassing, really."

I wasn't sure if I should laugh or just be impressed, a consideration that had me blinking several times in a row. That wasn't even a subtle one, just him bludgeoning the poor rude woman with a verbal club. The offender didn't know what to do either, sputtering before excusing herself. As she did, though, the elven ambassador turned to the green girl and winked, something at least half a dozen people here had to have seen.

With no other ideas, I looked to Rowenna for advice on this one; she understood the etiquette better than I did, and this was her party.

"Eh," my girlfriend said with a small shrug, whispering under her breath. "I never quite liked her anyway."

"Rubbing off on all of us," I muttered in an equally low voice. "Not sure if that's a good thing or a bad one."

I had no idea how he heard me, but I suspected he did, for the white-haired elf took that moment to chuckle into his drink like a bad movie villain. At least someone was having fun.

CHAPTER 7

LEAVING HOME

All good things must come to an end, and so, too, did my break for training. Rowenna had to return to her school, my school reopened—though I wouldn't be attending—and things began to return to some semblance of normalcy. Sure, much of the city was still a wreck, but the nobles were slowly leaving, and it was time for me to follow.

The ship that would be taking us to Elazia was, in fact, from that particular continent, and unlike our own vessels. Rather than looking like a steam ship powered by magic, it resembled something more akin to a floating fortress. The vessel wasn't quite as big as the old aircraft carriers from Earth, not that I'd ever personally seen one, but it was massive, and teeming with what looked like weapons.

"Heavens, is all that really necessary?" I said to my teacher.

"You've never traveled on the open ocean, have you? Only nearer to shore, I suppose. Not a lot of people do, for various reasons, but yes, it is necessary."

"It can't even come into the harbor properly," I pointed out, motioning at the smaller boat we needed to take to get to the ship.

"Eh," he dismissed. "Shouldn't you be saying your goodbyes?"

"Hmm?" I turned to see my mother approaching behind us, looking worried. How had he even known she was here?

I went to her. Mother looked . . . better. After my father's death, she'd been a bit reclusive for a time, which was odd to me. They weren't ever lovey-dovey, at least in front of me, but there'd been much I'd clearly missed. After looking lost for several days, she just looked simply, painfully sad.

"Hello, son," she said with a small smile. "I don't suppose you'll decide to cancel this?"

"No," I confirmed. "There's still more going on, and I want to know what and why."

"You could leave that to others, and stay here instead."

"I could," I agreed. "But I won't. There's no chosen hero here like in all those children's stories, no special person to save the world, or stop some disaster, and I'm certainly not such a person. What I am, though, is the person who's here, and someone who can do something, so I will."

Was I chosen? Honestly I didn't think so, not as some superhero. My abilities were thoroughly average, even for someone with magic. Sure, I was good at making guns and small machines, but I wasn't some overpowered monster capable of fighting demon kings or gods. No, I was just a man, a man who could only do so much. That was no excuse, though, to do less than what I could.

And what I could do now was find out why. Why had people come to kill Archmage Penumbra? What was their plan, their motive, their purpose? People had theories, perhaps a few good ideas, but that wasn't enough. The theories didn't even explain why they'd gone after the goblins so much, which was truly weird.

There was more still, though. Some of their actions had undoubtedly put pressure in places that may well have caused my father's death, and I wasn't about to let that go. Vengeance was a fool's errand, but justice wasn't, and someone out there had been doing some unjust things. So, I'd see if I could find them and bring them out of the shadows and into the light. When that happened, I had a feeling that my new acquaintance might have his own say.

"You're wrong," she said, pulling me out of my thoughts.

"About what?"

"There is someone chosen. You, son." A small smile played on her lips. "You chose yourself, and personally, I think that's a bit better than some of those stories. I just want you to know that you don't have to, and if you ever want to stop, you can."

"I love you too." She playfully hit my arm. "And I have a request."

"Oh?"

"I know you have feelings about it, but look after Kaylee for me. She may not be your daughter, but she's still my sister, and she needs all the help she can get."

Mother frowned, but after a sigh and a shake of her head, she said, "Very well, I'll keep an eye on her, and if I think she's in over her head, I'll do something. Don't expect me to baby her, though."

I could hear the boatmen calling us to disembark, but before I could leave she held onto me, pulling me down so she could kiss my forehead.

"You'll have to follow my request, though," she said. "Come home to me, safe."

"I'll do my best," I promised.

Too soon, I had to pull away, hop into the small loading vessel, and sail out to the larger ship. I waved at Mother, smiling as best I could, as we pulled away. Sure, the ambassador and I were prepared, but we still had much to do before we made it across the ocean, something I'd never done before.

Once we were all aboard the big ship, and our luggage was being brought on board, I was called to the councilor's chambers.

His room was large, stately, not opulent, but like something made for a military officer, with a desk and plenty of writing materials, along with a few chairs. His clothing was still in boxes, pushed against one side where a door to what must be his bedroom stood. There were other boxes, too, though, large ones sitting all about.

"You needed something?" I asked.

"Yes, we had some operational concerns before we left, but I had a conversation with your goblin friend, Sasha."

"Oh?"

"Indeed, and she wanted us to take something with us that you haven't yet been informed of. Now that we're underway, our security is quite a bit more potent, so I thought I'd share it with you."

"And what is—" I didn't finish before the lid of one of the boxes all but exploded off, a small green form shooting upward.

"Surprise!" said a familiar girl, goggles whirring as they adjusted to something or other. It was the same one who'd fought me several times, and gotten the better of me too.

"What the hell!" I shouted.

The councilor doubled over in laughter, wheezing as I looked between the two of them.

"A-ha-ha-ha, your face!"

"You could have told me about this!" I shouted at the old bastard.

"But then you wouldn't have been so surprised!" he said, still laughing.

"Not at all," Greta agreed, as she clumsily climbed out of her box. I couldn't help but notice the odd lack of grace, and it took a moment to register why.

"Are you pregnant?!" I asked the goblin girl with the visible bulge in her abdomen.

"Indeed, and I want my child to be born in our old homeland, so I decided to tag along. It will be nice to see where my people are from, anyway. Your friend only required that I play along with his joke."

"But it's only been . . ."

"Our gestational period is far shorter than that of humans."

"You're both such a headache," I grumbled, turning and leaving. They could have their fun with each other, if they were going to be like that.

CHAPTER 8

SEAS AND ISLANDS

With little else to do and few places I could reasonably go, I spent much of the journey studying language in an intensive way. This, of course, led to a certain goblin girl joining along with my lessons, because she, too, was bored.

"I cannot think we not allowed to see ship . . . insides?" she tried, struggling with the foreign words and grammar.

"No, I cannot believe they won't let us see the internals either," I agreed, subtly correcting her. We both spoke in the southern dialect. Practice makes perfect, after all.

"Bah, you're both allowed to visit some of the parts of the ship," our teacher pointed out from his nearby desk. He sometimes added in comments or corrections if he thought we needed adjustment in our speech.

"Not the guns," I said. Interestingly, the word *guns* was the same as in English; I'd been informed that it was in all of the elven dialects.

"Yeah!" Greta agreed.

"Much as I find you two amusing, I'm not letting you see what are undoubtedly military secrets that you might export to your own countries. Same for the engines, before you can bring that up. The elevators were at least fun for you two."

I laughed. "Why exactly is it you don't care about elevators?"

"Because the one who invented them was very specific about how they were made, and shared the information on how to make them with everyone. If there were some in the human lands, and there might be—I honestly don't know—we'd happily share our designs and maintenance protocols." Trying to translate the words *maintenance protocols* was a bit strange. It sounded almost like "cleaning and fixing times," only more formal.

"That's a bit strange, isn't it?" Greta pointed out.

"His Majesty became deeply irritated by people doing it wrong and would absolutely drill people who did. It stuck around in governance, even after he left."

"After he left? You make it sound like you were there, but that was very long ago, was it not?" Greta asked, seemingly confused.

"It was, and I do, don't I?" The councilor didn't elaborate, and it was clear from his tone that he preferred the topic dropped.

"I'm still surprised you brought a whole warship for this," I said.

"Sea monsters are no joke," he pointed out, happy to change the subject.

"That bad?"

"Some are larger than this vessel, and many of them have extremely potent magical abilities. Fish and octopi the size of buildings, sharks that can rip smaller boats to shreds, and even predatory whales that can control the weather are only a few. Even I don't think I've had a full cataloging of them in all my time. New ones pop up often enough that the depths must still have secrets."

"Should I be worried?" Greta inquired.

"No, none could destroy this ship so easily, and with me here, there is little danger. There are things in this world that can defeat me, but not many. Even if we did find such an enemy, they'd prefer to go for easier prey."

Eventually, conversation petered out, the day wore on, and the time had come for me to rest once more. So, I made my way to my assigned quarters, a room of steel panels and simple furniture, bolted down to the floor so as not to move with the gentle swaying of the ship. I thought to write some letters, knowing that most couldn't be delivered until well after I left Elazia, but I knew my family would still want to hear how I was doing.

My desk was . . . well, in some ways nicer than the one I had at home. It was functional, very basic, but decorated well. Gentle curves touched every surface, with small carvings on the legs and sides in some geometric pattern. The pieces were so tightly fitted together that there seemed to be no seam, and there might not be, if it were magically grown. Basic, but still a piece of art.

Everything on the ship was sort of like that. It was all functional, and not covered in needless bits, but all still subtly beautiful. Designs were present, but toned down, lacking any ostentatiousness, no odd sculptures or ceiling fixtures. No, each item looked like it had been made for a function, not to be shown off, but they had so many small details that stood out when looked upon, adding a simple beauty.

The way the ship ran was much the same too. Each of the crew seemed to know their jobs so well that it seemed effortless, intrinsic. This didn't mean that they slacked off, though. No, they were still disciplined, still watching for anything to go wrong and reacting quickly when it did. Practice. That was it. They were practiced until each was a master of their craft.

I'd known very few elves. Other than my grandfather and the ambassador, there were basically none in our lands. Here, though, I started to get an inkling of their culture. Long lives meant that their masters eclipsed ours by a high degree, and those that humans considered experts were adepts for some of them.

Every mechanic on this ship would be in charge on a human ship—the old man who knows what the engine is doing just by its sound and the vibrations in the water, the savant whose advice would always be heeded. But it was like that for every single job. The cooks knew their craft like five-star chefs, the sailors read the sea like a book. It was in its own way beautiful, planned, routine to them, but also seemed rigid.

I wrote of this, and as the days went by, other things too. Humans were clearly behind on magic, as these people used it for almost everything. The ship itself was packed full of magical items, not just technology, because each of the crew seemed to have at least a bit of mana. In Exion, they'd have been called talents, but here they were just another elf.

While deep in study of a small enchanted lamp, examining the many ways they'd used to squeeze more function and efficiency out of it, I was disturbed. Someone knocked on my door to tell me the councilor wanted me to come up to the deck to see something.

"What's going on?" I asked, looking out into the thinning rain. It had been pouring for days at this point.

"We should be approaching the goblin island now. My understanding is that this storm sort of covers it all the time. Thought you might want to see," he informed me. Greta was already there, looking through some spyglass she'd found.

Sure enough, before long, the clouds slowly cleared, the storm falling back behind us. I expected an expanse of green, but no such thing greeted me. Instead, there was nothing but bare rock, pock-marked oddly here and there, with darker patches in circles upon it. Craters, like from some vast attack, like something from the history books showing no-man's-land.

"What's happened?" I asked.

"Something unpleasant," the councilor said, frowning deeply.

"Another ship," Greta called, pointing.

"Ours," he informed her. "We'd planned to meet here, but there should be vegetation. The reports said . . ."

"What about the goblins? Where are they?" she asked, fearfully, to which the rest of us could only frown.

CHAPTER 9

EMPTY ISLAND

We did not bother meeting up with the other ship's crew before heading to shore. A certain goblin was very, very insistent that we see what was left. It was hope, but from what I could see, that hope was likely for naught. The only green was upon the shore, strands of kelp that had washed up. Not a blade of grass remained, and that was both terrifying and rather impressive.

"Father told us that there were caves," Greta said. "We must find them. Should any of our people have survived, they'll have hidden there."

"Greta . . ." I began.

"No, first we find them, then we discuss. I remember the stories, where they stood near the rocks, the entrances hidden. If I just follow his directions . . ."

She was almost frantic, babbling quickly. The councilor said nothing, letting her go, letting her work it out on her own. Perhaps that was the better way. I wasn't sure, but for once he made no jokes or quips, and that bode poorly. I let her pull forward, running along a cliff face as I got closer to him.

"This was done with artillery," I said, looking at the craters everywhere, huge ones, but some very subtle.

"Yes, then finished with magic, the land scoured. Bombard first, then fire and death to wipe it clean."

"You've seen it before?"

"Not often, but when we wanted to wipe something clean, fully exterminate some magical plague or creature, this is how we did it. If there are any left, and I doubt there are, they'll be hidden deep, and we'll need to rebuild the ecosystem on this island from scratch for them."

"You'd do that?"

"I may be a bit of a bastard, but I'm not without decency. At any rate those goblins will need a homeland. Your people are likely to want them gone soon, and exterminating a race of sentient beings doesn't sit well with me."

"Wouldn't have expected this from you . . . though I guess you've been through a lot before."

"Something much like this has happened before. I wasn't there to put things right that time, but I won't miss my chance this time."

It took her time, but eventually Greta did find the entrance to one of the tunnels. She hurried down it, heedless of any further danger. Of course, according to her, none of her kind would dare hurt one of their own who was with child, not that I thought they could beat her, anyway, but still.

The shaft went deep into the earth, much farther down than I'd thought anyone sane would build, but these warrens were ages old and supposedly often very full. Space may well have been a concern. It also gave hope, though, for if they were this far below the surface, the bombardment shouldn't have killed them.

The walls were wet and slick in places, the floor much the same, with the only light being from the two spellcaster's magic. Down we went, farther and farther until we came upon an opening. Cold coals were near the door, long burned out, the power of flame having left the small, makeshift firepit long ago. This room was where we found them.

All across the floor were bodies in various states of decay. Some were little more than bones, others nearly whole, but desiccated and dried somehow. There were no rats, insects, or anything else to rip and tear them apart, so they lay there, dead and gone.

Greta didn't have words, instead falling to her knees and weeping, surrounded by the corpses of her long-lost kin. It was a harrowing sound, pained and full of suffering, the scream of agony between the wails.

After a time she settled, still kneeling there, exhausted, weak, unable to continue.

"I am sorry for your loss," a calm, almost kindly voice said from the shadows.

It was another elf, one who could have been the councilor's brother. Long white locks flowed over his robes and framed his all-too-familiar face. I knew him, I'd met him, and he was here.

"Did you do this, are you the one responsible!" Greta accused, rising with a snarl.

"No, I did not, not this time."

"You will tell me everything you saw!" she spat, tossing forward her hands. From them sprang ribbons of light and magic, reaching toward the newcomer.

Before they could touch him, the spell dissolved, falling apart like smoke on the wind. I recognized the technique, if not the power. It was magical resistance, and he had just used it to unwind her magic like a wind blowing it to bits.

She didn't take that well. Greta threw several more projectiles at him. They wouldn't have even bypassed my magical resistance, poorly constructed and not very powerful. The elf just looked at her with tired eyes.

"I am not your enemy; now cease this," he told her, clearly not willing to raise his voice. "I would hate to have to restrain you, as my own people always loved children and loathed putting them at risk, but I will if I must."

"Why?" she asked, voice breaking on the word.

"That is something I intend to find out. Return above and rest for now. There will be much to do later. Boy, stay with me. We've much to discuss."

She did as he told her and left, helped along by our other elven companion. He didn't argue either, just took her arm gently and walked her back to the surface.

"You're like me," I said in English.

"Yes, the first of us that I know of to come to this world. Much like you, and Alana, and this Father, and a few more I've known over the years too." His language matched mine, perfectly pronounced, like he'd stepped out of a portal from Earth just yesterday.

"And what is it you want from me? I'm afraid if you want me to kneel, I already have a ruler in this world."

"I left my throne behind long ago, child. No, I want your help, for someone killed my friend, and I want to know who is responsible, and why. I even suspect that they had something to do with this massacre, too, heaping another crime upon their backs. Something is festering, and it stinks, stinks in a way I don't care to see again."

"And should I find the source of the mess?"

"Then we will cut away the rot."

CHAPTER 10

✶

NEW LIFE

"You knew the archmage?" I said after a long silence.

"Yes, for quite some time. It was very refreshing to meet one of us who would live so long . . ." He smiled and took a moment before saying under his breath, ". . . that wasn't my enemy."

"I only met her once, but she seemed nice."

"A bit silly at times, perhaps a bit overconcerned with duty as she aged. Who isn't like that though? I spent far too long trying to make others happy. Let me warn you as someone who's seen it, don't do that. It will only make you miserable, and you'll suffer from your losses more than you can imagine."

"Right . . . anyway, I'm all for going after whoever killed her, if only because our country views it as something like an act of war."

"It may well have been. I'm fairly sure it was the southern elves, but I'm not sure how deep their rot goes. It could be a breakaway faction, some black ops group gone rogue, or it could be from the top down, and that's what I want you to find out."

"You could probably find out yourself," I pointed out.

"I've made a few inquiries, but someone who can act more openly is needed. If I show up publicly anywhere on the continent, it would be a political upheaval, the likes of which I am loath to cause. For all that I dislike it, I've become something of a legend, you see."

"And you think anyone would even recognize you? Where have you even been all this time?"

"Plenty would," he said. "Some even believe I'm still around, though most think I'm dead. As for your other question, keeping to myself."

"Fine, fine. You said you were going to cut away the rot. Before I agree to help you, I want to know exactly what you mean."

"It depends on what you find, of course, but provided I see evidence, I'll remove the cause of all this is. If it is one individual or some small group, I'll just kill them. If it's the whole government, well, I've destroyed those before. Have to admit that doing so without being noticed will be harder though."

"What about Greta," I asked.

"What about her? I've nothing against her personally. Sure, I might have had to do something about that 'Father' had you not, but it sounds like that all worked itself out in the end." He shrugged. "Honestly, had you not done something, the priests would have. Busybodies, every one of those Orders, but they do keep order."

"Will you help the goblins rebuild?" I asked. "As a favor to me."

"I don't think that's wise. I can lend them a bit of support from the shadows, maybe ask for a warship to stick around so that what happened doesn't again while they put together their society, whatever that will be, but too much could have great unintended consequences. Maybe bring some plants here or something, sure, but not much more than that."

"Fine, I can live with that. Still, I can't believe someone would go this far," I said with a shake of my head.

"Me neither, and for no apparent reason. Sure, I'll believe that the creatures were bad enough here, based on the reports I've heard, but they were contained, and no real threat to anyone."

We chatted for a bit longer about what had happened, but there was nothing more of substance to say. He wanted revenge; I wanted justice and to protect my people. Greta probably wanted revenge, too, but she was with the councilor, whose name I still didn't know. Everyone seemed to be on the same side, even if that side wasn't very chipper.

"Well then, I'll be off. Mind if I ask you a question before I go?" I inquired.

"Not at all."

"Why didn't you ever make planes? Or cars, or anything like that?"

"Oh, well that wasn't really a huge interest of mine on Earth, so I would've been building from scratch. Dirigibles were easier when I started, and by the time I would have made any of the others, I could teleport, so no point. I'll admit to being curious as to what people would make without my input. Sadly, disappointed on that one."

With a huff of laughter, I left him, heading toward the boat. Naturally, fate conspired to keep me from getting back to my cabin so easily.

Greta, probably effected by stress, had gone into labor on the beach. She was ardently refusing to return to the boat, and seemed to be ready to snap at anyone nearby.

"My people here are dead, my child *will* be born on these shores. I won't let whoever did this take our island from us!" she growled at the councilor.

"You know you could die here, right?" he asked.

"I don't care!"

"Fine." With a wave of his hand he sent a series of light signals, and then somehow formed an odd-looking chair from the dirt itself. "Sit," he told her. This is a good position for what you seem determined to do. At least for most things that share our general anatomy, it is . . ."

"What would a male know of these things?!" she snapped, still angry.

"I have aided in the births of more children than you've met. Now sit down!" He seemed to be losing patience with her. I could not make such a boast, so I stood off to the side.

The old elf led her through a series of breathing patterns and examinations that sounded good, not something I was at all qualified to judge. Then, a small medical team came from the boat. The councilor even made some hot water in a bowl for something and aided the medics when they came.

After a few hours, during which time I was hiding away from the screaming goblin girl, I was told she'd had a son. The first of the new generation for this place. He even had an aura, I was told, one like clouds and rainstorms. If that held with what I knew, at least he wasn't one of us.

CHAPTER 11

✶

FOUNDATION

"Found another one," I announced to the small group who'd come with us, pointing at a tiny plant that was trying to survive in the barren soil.

We were taking a week, and only one, to stop and do reclamation on the island. I was a bit surprised that the elves were so invested in such a thing, being that they seemed more industrial than standard fantasy elves, but they saw the value in trying to preserve the local ecosystem, or at least what was left of it. To that end, we were scouring the whole place for every seed, every shoot, anything that survived the bombardment that might be helpful.

It was distasteful, but someone had opened up the bellies of the dead goblins. After all, they'd no doubt eaten some of the vegetation, and if there were seeds in their guts, those could be useful too. Everything was being handed over to a priest, who was doing what he could to grow the plants, but it wasn't going to be a fast process.

Carefully, I got a small flag I'd brought along and marked it. I didn't want to move and potentially damage the plant.

"You're surprisingly good at this," one of the soldiers said.

"I've got good eyesight; hearing too. Shame that I don't hear anything but us here. The people who did this were thorough."

"Yes, indeed." Most of the soldiers who spoke my tongue were extremely formal, though as it wasn't their first language, that shouldn't strike me as too odd.

"Why though? Perhaps they hated the goblins for some reason, but the animals? The plants? Seems excessive."

"Wanted to make sure that even if any survived, they didn't have anything to eat. At least that's what one of the officers said when we discussed it this morning. Something always survives, though, even if it's just a few small plants here and there."

This wasn't my forte. Even if I liked nature, it wasn't like I spent much time in it. There were no machines or mechanisms here, only barren soil and sprigs of growth. Neither did I think it would work completely. No, the whole ecosystem was gone, and there'd be no rebuilding all of it. The best we could try for was saving a few of the species that were left and potentially bring in something similar from elsewhere, though nobody here could even describe what was lost, and some of it was almost certainly unique.

"This place will never be the same," I said to him as I moved on, continuing to scan the soil.

"No, but it can be something. At least, I hope so. We'll do what we can, and then maybe call in some people from the mainland to get to the business of actually fixing it."

"Have to do something about the soil too. No roots with the wind and rain? It'll be carried off before too long."

"Make a note when we get back, in case someone hasn't already thought of it," he advised.

Greta was back on the ship, having ceded most of the operation to others. Physically, she was fine, taking care of her child and focusing all her energy on him. Mentally, though, I worried. Postpartum depression was common enough here, but they hadn't seen their ancestral homeland and most of their species wiped out. Greta was very clearly going through a lot. I didn't see her much, the girl having mostly retreated to her quarters and holing up there. What should have been a happy time for her had been reduced to something horrid and destructive.

As the sun set and our teams returned to the boats, I went to see her. It wasn't hard to locate her on the small vessel. I was glad to see that she'd made her way to one of the decks, where she sat with her child by a small window.

"We've found quite a few species of plants on the island, and they're being regrown quite fast. You can come and see tomorrow, if you want," I told her when I sat down, not really sure where to start.

"Perhaps, perhaps not. I find that place . . . distressing? Yes, I think that's the right word." Her voice was quiet, reserved.

"I know, I'm sorry. There will be help for you and yours, at least. The elves seem dedicated to that."

"Their leaders feel responsible, and told me as much. Did you know all of their countries used to be united under the Atali leadership? They broke away slowly as time went on, wanting their independence, and they were allowed to. Seems like their leaders view this as something their children have done."

"I'm bad at this, you know."

"You're trying, and that's something," she replied, not even looking at me.

"Do you think it's okay for me to leave you here with them? Your sister and mine are friends, and I'd feel bad if something happened to you."

She chuckled. "I don't think they mean me ill. Now that he's gone, I see it, how Father manipulated us, always withholding his help and affection, only giving it to those who did what he wanted. These elves are weird, and dangerous, but they're not like that. They don't really want anything from me. Condescending, but I don't have anything they need. So, I don't think they're trying to manipulate me, at least." Her child awoke, making a few noises before she cooed and settled him down.

"You never told me his name," I said, looking at the little green baby.

"I haven't given him one yet. Still thinking on that."

The next day she did come to the island, looking at the small patches of green and the few flowers that had been magically boosted from the seeds and shoots we'd found. It wasn't much, but it was a beginning.

As we headed out to leave for the night, she moved up near me.

"I decided on a name."

"Oh?" I said.

"Yes, I will call him Aris. I think it's a good name."

"It's a wonderful name. I'm sure he'll grow big and strong."

"I'd like to ask your thoughts on another name too," she added.

"Name for what?" I asked.

"The island. We can't well just keep calling it the Island with Goblins, can we?"

"And what were you thinking we should call it?"

"Foundation." It was a rather simple name, but lots of names were like that. Often simplicity got lost as language drifted, but places stayed the same.

"I like it. If that's what your people want to call it, I'm sure nobody will object."

"We will, then. I'm sure my people will like it, and if they don't, too bad." That got a snort out of me. The playfulness creeping back into her voice was something I'd missed.

CHAPTER 12

MESSAGES

All things must end, as did my time with Greta and the island. I moved onto another, slightly-less-populated boat, and we set sail. My former companions had left me, unable to go where I was needed, or unwilling, though I surely wasn't alone.

First were the tutors, multiple, who were trying to drill into my thick head the last bits of elven grammar and vocabulary. They . . . made me miss my former teacher, and were neither as skilled at instruction, nor as interesting as I'd found him to be. Nevertheless, I persisted and found that the dialect I was learning was becoming easier by the day. Turns out that if people only speak to you in one language (except to correct your screwups) you pick it up pretty quickly.

Though there were other things that I was being drilled on too. Most of it was my cover, because I needed one. Humans, even ones with elven blood, were pretty rare in the various elven kingdoms, and I was going to stick out. Humans were not well liked in the land I was going to, with no small amount of propaganda being made to tell how we had "stolen the elven birthright" or some such nonsense.

To this end, it looked like they'd scored me something akin to a visitor's pass. I was a traveling youth, interested in my family's history and the greatness of my elven ancestors and their many works and culture. Following that end, there were all kinds of plans for me to travel around the country, with tour guides arranged to take me to various places, where the locals would show off things that had been built thousands of years ago and not matched since. They were very, very proud of their heritage, though didn't bother to grow it by any meaningful way in far too long for my opinion.

Sadly it wasn't likely I'd be able to score any real new tech for myself, since . . . well, they didn't really have much. The best these people had were ancient, or made from ancient designs, repeated but seldom improved. It was like marveling at a sword that was beautiful, from a people that were still living in huts in the modern age. It wouldn't take from what their people had done, but they were doing nothing but copying their ancestors.

"Don't bring that up in front of the southerners. They're very proud," my tutor warned me when I voiced that opinion. "And, frankly, it's insulting to all of us."

"It's not meant to be. You can all do better; everyone can do better."

"Even your people?" he asked with a raised eyebrow.

"Especially my people. Goodness, we'll get there, but it'll take time. Look how much we've changed in just the past few hundred years." I wondered why it was so slow, but then it struck me. It was magic.

Magic was a cheat code for society, letting us do things that even the people of Earth would have struggled with, but here, you just used magic. Healthcare? Magic. Transportation? Magic. War? Magic ruled there too. And, because it was so powerful, and how much one potent magic user could do on their own, innovators could be crushed by pure magical might.

"You're not wrong, but after a certain point we reached the limits of what we could with information. Without a better way to store data and use it, there is really only so far we can advance beyond small changes." He sighed. "And one mind just can't keep all that together in their head."

"A point, I guess, humans may not have reached quite yet."

"You will soon though," he pointed out. "On another note, these are for you alone."

The man pushed some small cylinders across the table to me, clearly some kind of magical items, but I'd never seen them before.

"They contain information, and your mana alone will be able to unlock them."

"How's that work?" I asked.

"State secret. Not even I know. Also, there may be additional protections, so follow the directions exactly, and only open them when you're alone. Just put some of your mana into the top there, and be on with it."

I took them, and he left, and then I began to think. The cores had to be the answer here. They were effectively massive data storage devices. In fact, every magical item was. There was no way, no way at all, that the directions for making magical effects were less than a coding language, and if there was a coding language, then you could make something like a computer, maybe not the best one, but decidedly better than what was bouncing around.

As soon as I realized this, I frowned. I knew a bit about coding, but I was no genius. While I might be able to make a few small things here and there, a full operating system was well beyond my abilities. Someone had to have tried, though, someone better than me. Maybe if I studied enough, I could cobble together, not a full computer, but something like an old information processing system—spreadsheets for spellcasters, or maybe something like presentations, slideshows inflicted upon an unknowing populace. Was I that evil though?

With a dark chuckle I entered my quarters and popped open the tubes. The first was full of rolled up papers, though fewer than I might have expected. Mostly directions on how to meet handlers once I arrived on Elazia. I was supposed to go to a certain bar near my hotel and wait, exchanging passwords with someone who would come. I sighed as I read the passwords. Someone honestly expected me to say such a thing?

After I memorized the instructions, I burned the papers and moved to the next cylinder. Just like with the previous one, I gripped it and ran a finger gingerly along the top, pushing just a bit of magic into it. The tube lit up, the top popped off, and a small horde of spring-loaded puppets flew from the top. It was far too slow to scare me, but it did throw little goblin-faced streamers into my face.

With a deep sigh I remembered that at least two of my nearest accomplices on this trip were effectively children. There was a note at the bottom, too, one small paper that fluttered away. With a frown I picked it up and began to read.

Greta suggested we do something like this before the whole finding all her people dead thing, and while she may not get to see it, we'll let her know her joke lived on. Kindly take it in the good humor with which it was intended.

A Friend

I sighed again, but without trying, I could feel the corners of my lips rise. Sure, they were stupid, but this wasn't wrong. He was doing this for a friend. How could I begrudge him that?

CHAPTER 13

★

SUNSET TALKS

Ship switchovers eventually had to happen, with nobody sane wanting a warship, even one from ostensibly an ally, landing in their ports. I could wax about the elven port cities that I moved through as we did this, about the skylines, about the many things I saw, but there really wasn't much to tell.

Most of the places that I ended up stopping were deep ports in small- or medium-sized cities, and I saw very little. Docks were docks—busy, congested, and full of unhappy sailors who really wanted to get their work done for the day. The shapes and designs of the other ships were different, some made of wood and in colors I wasn't quite used to, but the biggest difference was the food.

Once they managed to get me onto a local sailing ship, rather than a massive ocean-crossing monstrosity, I ended up getting to taste some of the local cuisine. It was largely tropical, with more fruits than I was used to, less vegetables, and very little bread to speak of. Instead we each got a very large fruit, which seemed to serve as the local equivalent to starch, melon-sized and roasted rather than fresh. Served with it was lots of fresh fish and more citrus than I was used to.

There were fewer herbs, overall, or at least not the same ones, but I was happy to see that tea was alive and well in this part of the world. It was different from what we had back home, but similar enough to clearly have come from the same plant at some point in history. There were more floral notes mixed with the brew, an altogether lighter style, though lacking in cream, which I commonly took my tea with. Unlike the herbs, though, there were several of what could only be described as spices that I wasn't familiar with, odd ones that I didn't have a word for.

It occurred to me at some point that much of what I found distinct would likely be very, very subtle for most people. My senses were enhanced, and while smell and taste certainly weren't the most potent, they were better than what most humans had. It was one of the odd perks of being a physical magic user. Things that were subtle, almost difficult to describe to me would likely be lost in the noise to others.

My training in language also moved from a classroom setting to more practical uses. As I got closer to the southern part of Elazia, I began meeting more people from there, mostly on or near the docks. My final ship was in fact a public one, and I got quite a lot of looks from basically everyone aboard.

"Good evening," I said to a fellow on one of the upper decks, as I made to watch the sunset.

"Oh? Oh, what an odd accent. Are you from the north?" he inquired.

"No, the human continent, though my grandfather is an elf."

"Truly? I've never met anyone who's been there, though I'm told it's rather poor. Most humans aren't . . . very civilized, are they? Um, nothing against you, of course. A child of our people could never be so."

"It's quite different," I told him. "Less magic overall, from what I've seen, and some of the technology isn't nearly as refined as some of what I've seen here."

"Of course, His Majesty was the most brilliant person to ever live! His genius is still unmatched in these waning days, no matter how hard we try to reach such heights. A goal to ever strive for."

"He certainly did quite a lot for people, didn't he?"

That was something else I'd come to learn about a lot of elves; they pretty much worshiped the old king. It was fervent, almost religious in nature, like he was a near-perfect man. This contrasted with what I'd seen—a brilliant, and certainly powerful, but withdrawn man, not some hero of legend devoted to righting all wrongs. I briefly wondered how they'd act if they knew he was still around.

"Oh, so much. It's a real shame that most of the old ancients won't come to join us anywhere near the southern nations. Which one are you going to, if you don't mind my asking?"

"I'm headed to Nicon," I said. "Hear there's quite a bit to see there. Lots of education and culture I'm excited to get a look at." And the rumors of military action, though this random man didn't need to know about that.

"Nicon? Nice city. That would be the Ergen Empire, then. Wonderful people there, and I'm sure they'd be happy to show you the greatness of your heritage. I'm heading to one of the outer states, bit more south than that."

"I'm guessing you've been there, then? I've only heard so much about it."

"Oh sure, the city itself is one of the oldest, if not *the* oldest, around. Even competing with Atal for that title, as they both show up in the earliest records and were both around when the king first rose. Atal is considered greater, but not by much."

"What's it like though?"

"Bountiful farmland on all sides, towering spires, all built around a multi-lobed lake of unimaginable size, almost an inland sea. It's beautiful, really, the shores so pristine and lovely, maintained so people can enjoy them. You know, it used to all be swamps, back in historical times."

"Really?" I asked.

"Oh sure, but you don't need proper irrigation and water control for long to fix that up, and once you have, you've got some of the best land for crops you've ever seen. Better. Some of those rivers and canals are quick and easy to navigate, with tours and the like for anyone who's interested in a more scenic time."

"Sounds like you've done that too."

"My parents used to drag us to some of those tours every year when I was a kid; made us sail around for days," he said with a laugh. "It was nice, good times."

We mused about childhood as the boat ambled along, though I never caught his name. It wasn't important to us to trade names. We were just two men talking about where we were going and where we'd been. I, of course, kept to what was the public story, but even with that, there was much to discuss.

The trains we had back home were of the greatest interest to him. For some reason he'd not known that we had such things. They weren't everywhere, though there were a few similar things here. It was something I could really get into without revealing too much. I'd loved trains as a child, and I still did; beautiful machines of magic and steel, a perfect blend of this world and my first. Sadly, there weren't any in the south at all. Boats were far more economical with the deep canals that served to move water about and irrigate everything.

That made me frown. It seemed I wouldn't get to see any elven trains on this trip.

CHAPTER 14

✶

MAKING IT ASHORE

Deep blue water lapped at the sides of the ship like a happy puppy as we slowly sailed into the port. The sun was shining high in the sky, and it was a near-perfect day. As our ship cut through the water toward the dock, I saw a number of people. They weren't just observing. They were mostly workers, sailors, and other deck hands, busy about their work like ants in their hive.

All around there was action as men pulled sea life of surprising size off of fishing boats, or rolled heavy barrels from ship to shore. There were other types of people too—assistants, friends of the passengers, and men to help unload passengers from our ship, so that the next batch could be brought on.

Luckily for me, I'd traveled light and could carry my own luggage. Of course, I could carry quite a lot, but I only had a couple of cases with me. It was enough for my purposes, with various books and extra things having been whittled down. At this point I didn't plan to do much more studying of the language other than through direct interaction, so having too many tomes on hand would be a bit of a pain.

The gangplank was easy to cross over the lapping water, and once more the brilliant blue of it struck me. I couldn't help but envy the people here. They had such a lovely shore, while the one back home had been rather lackluster, gray, and cold. There would be time to think about that later, and the heat—it was far warmer than I'd anticipated.

There was an immigration checkpoint here. Apparently, the people of this region took their security quite seriously, but the worker seemed pleased enough with my papers. I was also told in no uncertain terms that I needed to keep them with me at all times. While it seemed unlikely that anyone would question my presence, the authorities might, and then I would be detained if I didn't have them. That had already been covered in my briefings, so I was more than happy to oblige.

The Ergen Empire ran on a rather different system than I was used to, with various forms of transportation, all of which were new to me. There were small carts pulled by men or beasts, as well as trams, of all things. I wasn't sure how the latter worked, but I suspected the answer was magic. It generally was.

I tried, and failed, to make sense of the tram schedule, and since they were packed to the brim with people, I wasn't too disappointed. Instead, I hired a cart to take me to my hotel. I just had to give the man the name of the place and hope for the best, because I had only the vaguest idea of where exactly it was.

"First time here?" the man asked, looking back at me shrewdly.

"That obvious?"

"You're looking at everything around you," he said. "Locals don't. And the accent of course."

"Fair enough," I replied. "I'm a bit struck with how the city is laid out."

The city was denser than lead. The buildings were tall, taller than any back home in Exion, and there were people everywhere. It was all controlled chaos, with probably many hundreds of thousands in what was not even the largest city in this region.

"What about it?" he asked.

"It's all so dense—people living almost on top of one another. Are all cities here like this?" I inquired.

"Pretty much. You have to keep the city shields up to protect from monsters, a real problem on the rare occasion that they appear. Every now and then, villages are completely wiped out, so people like to live in the cities, where it's much safer."

"Oh, I see. While we have monsters on Hediza, I don't know of many that could kill a village." I'd used the local word for my home continent. There were few monsters back home. They were dangerous, but it would seem there were more here. "Do they shield the whole city?"

"Out to the walls. There's a few places that like to build outside them, but those are mostly the poor or the merchants trying to save a little money. Nobody thinks that's smart, but you can't stop some people. Believe me, if I told you how many I've told not to do this or that who went and did it, you'd be here all day, and we're nearly at your destination."

He pulled into the driveway of the hotel as he spoke, going up a winding incline to a large double door. There was a garden outside, small and simple but well landscaped, with a few small statues and various benches arranged throughout, and above it stood a several-story-tall building, light and inviting. I bid him good day and headed in, surprised at what I saw.

The inside was almost modern. There was a fan overhead, and a quick look told me it was powered by magic, and around the entry desk, fish tanks. This place could have been in any city on Earth, and aside from the staff's pointed ears, would have fit right in. A uniformed attendant spoke to me kindly and led me up a grand staircase. Large windows dominated, with another small sitting room near the top.

As we approached what was to be my room, a maid darted into the hall, standing aside after having clearly heard us coming.

"Is everything ready? You know the boss will be quite unhappy if he finds you slacking," the attendant said in a condescending manner to the girl.

"Yes ma'am," the maid said. "Everything is in order."

"Humph." With a wave, she dismissed the girl, who scurried off in a hurry.

"Apologies for her. She's . . . *thin* and still trying to figure things out." I recognized the word. It was a derision against those with little elven blood, and one that I, as a clear foreigner and wealthy man, was being overlooked for.

"It's fine, I'm sure," I responded.

"If anything isn't up to standard, let me know and I'll see to it that she's disciplined," the attendant offered.

"I shall," I lied in response, keeping my voice level with no small effort.

I'd been around servants and staff for most of this life, and I'd become quite good at reading them. In this case, however, it wasn't in the least bit hard. It was, in fact, painfully obvious. The maid was scared, terrified that she'd be found wanting. I'd seen it before in other people's maids, and my own family's staff when Mother performed her inspections, and it grated on me. Seeing people mistreated like that just rubbed me the wrong way, perhaps because it reminded me of my own dear sister.

The room was quite modern, like downstairs. Bed in the side room with large opening windows and a sizable fan. No fireplace, which in Exion would've been terrible, but here with the heat mattered little. There was even a small bathtub with hot and cold taps, all run by magic. It seemed that that would become a whole new thing to get used to.

After settling in, I waited until twilight and went to the bar where I was supposed to meet my contact. It was easy enough to find. I just asked the woman at the front desk, a different one, but no less happy to aid me.

The bar was clearly where locals congregated. Homey in comparison to where I might find myself back home, but I liked it. They had a number of drinks to choose from, mostly ciders made with berries I'd never heard of, and a cheerful staff. I received looks, of course. I stood out like a sore thumb in clothes that were clearly not from this region, but that was part of the whole charade.

"My, my, a foreign man here? How new," a sultry voice said from nearby. It was a woman just slightly below my own height, not standout beautiful, but very pretty. I knew the words at once, and smiled.

"And here I've not seen a woman with such wondrous assets in some time," I replied. "A surprise to me as well." It was the password I'd been given and one I would never have said myself, in either world. "Care to join me?"

CHAPTER 15

✶

THE SPY

The woman sat beside me and reached for a small ball on one side of the table, between the salt and pepper shakers. I'd personally thought it was just a decoration, but was quickly proven wrong. There was a fuzzy feeling for a moment and a light curtain covered the booth.

"Privacy ward," she told me with a smile. "Not foolproof, but something that good would be obvious, wouldn't it? This will keep others from hearing or seeing us." She must have noticed my surprise.

"Can't say I've seen one of those in a bar before . . ."

"Keeps the noise down when there are lots of people around, and is considered good form if you're meeting someone a little more intimately. At any rate, shall I presume you're Percival then?"

"I am, though I wasn't given a name for you."

"Call me Kitia, and not knowing things is part of why you're here, isn't it? Here to learn, here to observe."

It was clear from the way she spoke that Kitia, almost assuredly not her real name, was trying to keep from delving into actual secret information. If someone had heard what we'd said so far, it wouldn't be bad. Heck, I even had some documents that made it look like I'd corresponded with a few people here, or had introductions, at least. It wouldn't be out of the norm for me to know of one or two people.

"It is, though I'm not sure what I should be looking at," I admitted.

"Oh, good to know you're ready to get started on your work, then. There are some letters of introduction to local educational institutions. You worked on some of the mechanics and things back on Hediza, did you not? I think these will be very educational, and I hear they have connections with governmental officials who could show you the real wonders."

"Why, thank you. I'm quite excited to see what they have made."

This was all part of my mission too. I was to get close and see what I could see. The introductions were part of that. Things weren't like they were on Earth, with so much paperwork and red tape that making a false identity, or getting someone into odd places was neigh impossible. No, things were more fluid in this world, a result of not having computers.

Moreover, I was exactly the kind of person that would be desirable for the local government to attract. They were really proud of their heritage, so someone coming to visit was a boon to their pride. I had elven blood, something that we'd be playing up for them, too, and another point that would make them more apt to show me how great they were. A child returning home, welcomed by his elders. That's how they'd see me, as long as I didn't screw up.

There was also the fact that I was something of a mechanical prodigy back home. I wasn't famous per se, but I was well enough known in some circles. Grandpa and I had been going to various Royal Society meetings for years, doing presentations there, and then there was the plane. That invention was huge, and while the news had yet to spread too far, there'd surely be whispers. Wouldn't you want to wow someone with a hand in inventing tech, particularly if it reminded people of what your people made many years ago?

"A point though," Kitia said, interrupting my thoughts. "While being a foreigner will get you a bit of leeway, don't go starting fights or getting caught places you aren't supposed to be. The authorities here aren't to be trifled with, and you sincerely do not want to irritate them. They probably won't give you any trouble, so long as you're doing what you're supposed to, but they are quite strict."

"Not to worry; I seldom have issues with the authorities," I said, and winced. That wasn't entirely true, but I didn't have bad rapport with them, at least.

"Mmm hmm, my uncle's letters told me all about you, and your words when I came up weren't entirely polite either. You'll want to lay off of such bold declarations in the future. If it's someone you don't have a connection to, they will take offense." She wasn't buying that either. Fair enough.

"It was a suggestion from your uncle, as I'm sure you already know. Bit of a joker, isn't he?"

"Unfortunately so, and he does love to tease me about my proportions." She made a move that clearly indicated which ones she was referring to, and . . . well, she was very well-endowed.

"You have nothing further to worry about from me. I'm already taken, after all."

"Oh, really? Out there breaking girls' hearts already?"

"More complicated than that. Family friend whose parents have been trying to get us together for ages. She's lovely, too, and enjoyable to speak to. There's a lot of things she sees that I simply don't." I gave her a smile. I had a lot of compunctions about my relationship with Rowenna, but not respecting her wasn't one of them.

"The genius inventor not seeing things? Hard to believe."

"Being good at one thing doesn't mean you're good at everything, and I'm hardly a genius. A bit clever, perhaps. Perhaps a bit more clever than most, but I cannot claim a spot among the giants, nor would I want to. Those people seldom have happy lives from what I've seen."

"That's surprisingly deep, you know, mature."

"Thank you, I think . . ."

She laughed at me again, seeming to warm to the whole thing and giving a light shake of her head.

"I see now why my uncle sent you here. He may well be trying to set us up. Have to disappoint him, though, I guess." I personally doubted that, but it was nice to hear her say so. Then she got up suddenly, said goodbye, and left.

It hit me then. At least some of what she was saying was just an act. How much though? Clearly she'd kept it going because someone might be listening, no matter how unlikely that seemed. What did she really think though? Was I a naive child to her, or an asset? Honestly, I couldn't tell what was what, and perhaps that was the best part of her act. If she could fool me, who'd known who she was, then she'd surely fool anyone watching idly.

As I pondered that and finished my drink, I saw that she'd left her contact information. Probably the publicly known ones, somewhere I could go to talk to her if needed. I was going to have to get used to all the cloak-and-dagger stuff soon. Sure, I knew how to fight with an actual cloak and dagger; that had been part of my training, but actual spy craft? No, certainly not. It seemed almost an oversight, but maybe not knowing some things would be best for now. Who knew what tells might give a spy away, things I'd never considered.

Instead the only role I needed to play was, well, me. I was pretty good at being me. I'd been doing it for years. Now, I may be around very different people, but being myself wouldn't be difficult, and I'd had enough experience with mechanically-minded folks over the years that I was sure as soon as we got to chatting, things would work out fine.

CHAPTER 16

✶

SAYINGS OF THE ANCESTOR

I attended to my task, aiming for one of the closer places on the list Kitia had given me. This was a college of sorts, a technical one that focused on machines. I had some letters introducing me, and managed to arrange a tour of the public facilities without too much trouble. Elves loved to show off their stuff, but honestly, I wasn't terribly impressed.

"This is one of our newest pieces from the labs," the guide explained to me.

What he was showing me was mirrored several times through this hall, some of them labeled as hundreds of years old. It was an elevator, and it was weird to me that they seemed to put so much effort into them, but it didn't matter. The design principles were there, with small incremental increases in efficiency, or sometimes materials switched out, but the overall item, and underlying mechanics had stayed basically the same, for centuries.

"I see. And these extra pieces here . . . What do they change?" I inquired politely.

"Oh, yes, those. See, with this arrangement and a small change to the underlying enchantments, we can increase mana efficiency by four percent. Maybe that seems small, but it adds up! See, we put these all over, so every bit matters, and this is a significant improvement."

"That makes sense. How does it compare to the original model you have back there?" I asked, pointing to the first one as we chatted.

"A forty percent efficiency increase overall from the oldest ones we know of. Though most of the modern results are coming from material changes. Some of the older steel and iron models were fairly poor at the job. They were better than anything else at the time, of course, but not as good as we have now."

This seemed obsessive, almost mad, to me. How long had they been working on these? Why? I couldn't imagine men spending generations trying to work out kink after small kink on a design like this. It would be insane. They didn't, though, did they? Elves lived much longer than men did, so perhaps that was part of it.

"I think humans would just add combustion engines before spending so much time on the effort," I admitted with a frown.

"Bah! You know His Majesty told us about burning things for power, and do you know what he told us?" There it was—a fallback on a figure that had been gone for literally thousands of years.

"I do not," I admitted.

"That we should be careful of it. That too much would cause destruction and disruption of the world around us. I've been told that human cities have an ever-present layer of pollution, smog, and filth everywhere. Is that true?"

I crinkled my nose, remembering the first time I'd gone to Exion, and the horror of the nasal assault.

"Sadly, yes, the city I was living in before coming here was . . . fragrant."

"Yet have you seen such in one of our cities?" he asked like a teacher explaining something basic to a slow child.

"No, I suppose I haven't."

"That is because here on Elazia we use magic wherever we can, not engines, as much as we can get away with it. All of us, well, all real elves, have at least a little magic, and that little bit adds up. Of course, we don't want to waste it, so everything needs to run as smoothly as possible."

"I see, that's quite informative. Not sure it is helpful for humans, as so few have magic, but it is enlightening." I thought for a few moments, considering. "Are these mandates written down somewhere? I'm not sure I've seen such things written down anywhere."

"Oh yes, has nobody ever gotten you a copy of *Sayings of the Ancestor*? It's a must read for our educational system."

"I've never even heard of it. Probably one of those things that slipped through the cracks."

"*That* is a travesty, and one I'll be happy to remedy. Everyone should read it, know it; it's helped bring our society so far." I really was curious what was in that book, as he seemed to have an almost religious zeal for it.

"I'm sure it will be very revealing. Though, back to the question at hand, magic is used for all of these?" I asked.

"Hmm? Oh yes, because we all have some. You have magic, do you not?" His question was clearly one of interest, and his eyes narrowed as he asked it.

"Indeed, there is much elven blood in my family," I replied.

"Then you understand, don't you? Why we hate to waste our power?"

"I think so, yes."

The tour recommenced, and I continued to be a bit put off by his fervor, but it changed little. I even got a copy of the book. It was a fairly large thing, and was available at the institution's book store.

I was happy to note that here, at least, the pattern with my previous world didn't hold sway, with most volumes being reasonably priced, or even inexpensive. Coming from the world I had, where it was a running joke how expensive textbooks were, this was refreshing.

I gave one of the volumes they had on mechanics a quick look, but it became quickly clear that it was written in very formal, technical language. Trying to struggle through it would take me ages, and would probably end with a lot of misunderstandings that I was uninterested in, so I put it back. My sigh as I gave up on that one got a smile from one of the workers, but they were nice enough to help me with what I was here for, so I had no complaints.

The whole institution was almost jarring to behold, but it did bear fruit. While I was there I got another invitation to some mechanical demonstrations they were putting on, an altogether more important matter than my own questions and personal interests.

So, I returned to my hotel, book in hand, wondering why nobody had bothered to give me what seemed to be a foundational work for this society before getting here. The scared maid was there, and I nodded to her kindly as I passed, hoping to brighten her day a bit.

As I sat down to begin looking into the book, though, I found that it was . . . well, wild was one way of putting it. Whoever had written this, it was certainly not the man they idolized so much. I doubted whoever had written it had even met him. Each saying, and there were many, was referenced to a certain individual or a place he'd written something down, and almost all of them were lacking context. Instead there were pages trying to explain what would have almost certainly been offhand remarks, or notes scribbled in the margins of books.

There were so many examples, but the one I liked most was "Ignorance is not knowing, stupid is not wanting to know, stupid should hurt." This was seemingly uttered as a response to a question about why he allowed people who didn't try to get answers to suffer inconveniences and was used to justify so much. While it seemed too innocuous in context, it was put into motion for harsh punishments in schools should someone actively resist learning. Corporal punishment was even used, if it was to be believed, but the way out was clear too—effort. The book made clear distinctions between those putting forth effort and failing and those not putting forth effort—one was unfortunate, the other viewed as an insult.

As I read it I realized that the implications and explanations given for that sentence were three pages long, the details exhaustive, and exhausting to read. It was actually quite illuminating about their society. There were, of course, many others.

"I don't know: It's important to admit when you don't know something; no shame in it."

"Pride in yourself is for fools."

"Tools are for making people's lives better."

"Of course he did that; he's an asshole."

"Farmers are good folk."

"Huh, I was wrong. I've been wrong before, and I'm sure I'll be wrong again." This was the most divisive one, and had almost a whole chapter devoted to it.

CHAPTER 17

✶

A DIFFERENT MAID

While I'd thought my first meeting hadn't been ideal, apparently, the school's staff had felt very differently. My willingness to ask questions and "be corrected" was seen positively. The fact that I'd immediately bought the book of sayings by a man they were all fangirling over when it was suggested to me had gone over even better. I didn't know they'd actually taken an interest in that, but they had.

It was a casual level of inspection I hadn't suspected, but that I really should have. These people were obsessive over their work, and while I'd been in a very public place—a university—I should've expected everything I'd done to be looked at. It had been foolish of me to think otherwise, but luckily, I already fit the idea of what they were looking for in people from my lands. I had elven blood, which was an instant improvement, I was humble, which everyone everywhere tended to like in those they viewed as lesser than themselves, and I was genuinely interested in learning.

This meant that I had an in for more things like discussions in their equivalent of our own Royal Society. I wouldn't be giving any talks, but just getting in to listen was more than enough. Gains would be incremental, not all at once. That was simply the nature of these things. However, I had something else I wanted to look at while I was here.

"Hello there," I said to the maid as she came by to clean the room. "How are you?"

"Oh!" she said with a small start. I didn't look up from the papers I was leaned over. "I, um, I'm well sir. Very well indeed."

"That's good to hear, very good. I hate to impose, but I've heard some things recently that I'm not quite clear on. Would you be willing to help me with that?"

"I'm not sure that I'm really the best person for that, sir. Perhaps one of the front desk people would be better?" she tried, clearly eager to get away.

"No, I think they'd give me a less clear answer than you, or would otherwise deflect. It won't take long, and I assure you it will improve my opinion of both this hotel and your work overall."

I hated myself for doing this, but I'd already seen her fear of the receptionist. What would happen if I complained? I had an idea that it would be very, very bad for her, and she knew that. It was, of course, an empty threat. I'd never do such a thing to some innocent girl, but she didn't know that. As I saw the visible wince and tightening of her frame, I knew I had it.

"Yes, sir," she acquiesced.

"Thank you. I heard someone refer to others as 'thin,' but I'm not perfectly clear on what that means exactly. Could you explain it to me?"

"It-it has to do with how much human blood someone has," she said with a gulp. "It's rather important."

"How important?" I asked, looking directly at her.

"Incredibly, sir," she said, lowering her eyes.

"And what level makes someone *thin* then?"

"It . . . sort of depends on who you ask. The government cutoff is ten percent, though a lot of places now are looking at fifteen or twenty as their baseline. Below that, and it's almost impossible to find a job, and the authorities . . ." She didn't finish.

"They keep records of genealogy?" I asked.

"Yes, though there's testing too. All citizens have to go through it."

"And if you're too thin?"

"That's very bad, sir, very, very bad."

"I see. If you don't mind my asking . . ."

"I'm at eleven and a half percent. If I get fired from this job, it's possible I won't be able to get another, and with my current percentage, the law would look poorly on me. Please don't complain. I'll do . . ."

"You don't need to do anything, dear, and have no worries; your work has been exceptional and you've been quite helpful. I doubt you want me to tell your bosses directly, but I'll compliment the cleanliness and excellent staff to one of the higher workers before I leave." Having gotten the straight answers that I wanted, there was no reason to cause her any further stress.

"Thank you," she said with a tiny voice.

Before she left, I asked one more question.

"Why don't you leave?"

"Um . . . getting travel papers can be . . . difficult."

"Oh, I see. My apologies."

As she scampered away, I began to worry. How bad were things here? There were a number of different societies from Earth that had had this kind of thing. There'd been caste systems, segregation, and all other manner of separations, some quite brutal indeed, but I didn't know what I was dealing with here. There'd even been whole groups that had been rounded up and put through reeducation or other terms that mostly meant genocide. Her reactions did tell me one thing, though. It was probably on the more harmful end.

There was also the evidence that they'd killed our strongest archmage, a clear act of war. It was an opening act, one to weaken, but did this land have other plans? If so, then they weren't just looking at me as someone interesting, but as a potential collaborator. That was the role I'd need to play.

None of my thoughts could be written down, but I had deep worries. If they were like this to their own, what would they be like to people who were wholly human? Not good. Second class citizens, at best, slaughtered at worst, but probably somewhere in between, based on what I was seeing, and some of their weapons were better than ours.

Still swirling these things around in my head, I headed back downstairs, stopping at the reception desk. The one manning it today was a slightly older man, and very proper looking.

"Something wrong, sir?" he asked.

"Just wondering if you might suggest somewhere to eat, as I'm still rather unfamiliar with the area. Everything here has been wonderful so far; quite well maintained, very clean."

"Of course, sir. I understand. If you find your room in need of any further cleaning, please let me know and I'll arrange it." The smile on his face, half there and vicious, told me exactly what he meant by it.

It took all of my long years of schooling my face not to frown, or rip his head off. I'd have to apologize to my grandmother. It seemed noble education was good for something.

"Certainly, I will," I told him, knowing well I'd never be requesting *that* service.

"Now, as for places to eat, there are a number of excellent ones nearby." He began to list a few, but I wasn't really paying attention, instead focusing on the terrible signs I'd gleaned from our conversation.

CHAPTER 18

✶

LORAN

Two weeks of keeping my head down, of listening to people talk, of attending various exhibitions and shows, and I finally felt like I was getting somewhere. I was at a party the likes of which I'd not been to before.

The man who was showing me around had only introduced himself briefly as Holsten. He was a cheery enough fellow about his task.

It was much larger, much more open, but it was a party, and I'd trained for this. So, I mingled, mostly keeping quiet and listening to what people were saying. Honestly, the majority of the conversations were pretty bland; it typically was during these types of events.

And then I saw someone I knew, at least in passing. The man from the college who'd told me about the book I'd bought.

"Why, hello again," I greeted him. "I didn't know you were going to be here."

"Nor I you, though I'm quite happy to see you're here."

"Glad to hear. I don't believe I got a chance to properly thank you for your book recommendation." Of course we both knew that he knew and that I knew that he knew, but that was beside the point. It was just polite.

"Indeed, indeed. It's wonderful to hear that you liked it."

"And which book would this be?" asked a voice from near us.

I turned to see another elf approaching, older if I was to judge, and perhaps with more elven blood too. It was hard for me to tell, but I was starting to see some of the subtle differences in the ears and certain facial features. There was, also, the way they held themselves, with this man giving off an aura of seriousness. His military uniform helped with my assessment, with crisp lines and perfect arrangement from top to bottom.

"*Sayings of the Ancestor*. Did you know they don't teach it in Hedıza?" the professor asked him.

"It is true," I said with a nod. "At least as far as I know, it wasn't on any of our reading lists."

"Well, that's a shame. Something we might well endeavor to fix," he replied with a smile. "Tell me, what did you like about it?"

That was a question I hadn't been expecting, but could easily answer.

"While most of the sayings had a very serious tone, some clearly held both wisdom and jest, if I'm understanding them correctly. That shows forward thinking, knowing that people would find it . . . funny, and then think about what was being said. It opens the way for discussion and inspection that a drier comment might have let fall away." It was even part of the local theorizing on some of them, not just something I myself felt, so I doubted it would cause offense.

"And the advice itself?" he questioned.

"Practical. Much of it is quite obvious in retrospect, but a lot of things are like that. It takes someone saying them, and making sure you hear them for the words to really lodge in properly. Without that, many will fail to heed what should be simple. Yet he puts it in a way that even children can glean knowledge from."

A lot of Sun Tzu was like that, and his work was still popular back on Earth last time I was there. Saying that if your enemy sees no escape except through you and will die otherwise means they'll fight tooth and nail to go through you is pretty damn obvious, but having someone point that out helped.

"Well said," the military man said with a smile before holding out his hand. "Commander Loran. Good to see you're doing so well here."

"Percival Shadestone. A pleasure to make your acquaintance," I replied with a nod, taking his hand. Handshakes were a thing here, probably because of someone I'd met, if I had to guess.

"You know, I think I've heard of you." That was not at all surprising. He'd probably been told all about me before I'd even been invited to this event. "I'm told you were the one who made a flying machine."

That was not supposed to be public knowledge.

"My grandpa built it, if I'm being honest, though I did aid him where I could. He'd apparently heard of His Majesty's flying machines in his youth and is quite skilled when it comes to making things." All of those things were true. Grandpa had actually paid for building the thing, and he was very well regarded in our lands.

I needed to downplay my part here, and I thought I was succeeding. People really weren't supposed to know that I knew how to build planes, and if they did, then I might soon find myself in a lot of trouble. It seemed to work though. While they were all still interested, they weren't looking at me like I was a genius.

"I see, I see. He based it off of one of those, then?" Commander Loran asked.

"I'm not quite sure, though it wouldn't surprise me at all. I only ever did some of the work on the edges, though, and didn't help with the magical propulsion. There's probably something important with that you'd need, but he did that design himself."

The cat was already out, and I had no fear for Grandpa. He could take care of himself. Right here, right now, I needed this man to believe that I wouldn't be much help to him, because I couldn't be much help to him.

"Unfortunate. I had really hoped to see one."

I gave a small smile. "I am young still, Commander. Perhaps soon we'll see them flying here."

He grinned back, a toothy, unpleasant thing. "That would be lovely, indeed, particularly seeing the work of one of ours brought home to us. We've lost so much, and I so desire for it to be found once more. That's the way of things, isn't it? That we should desire to improve ourselves always, but still take joy when the lost return?"

"A wonderful point, sir," the professor said, patting me on the shoulder.

I didn't know which part of what I'd said had done the trick, but whatever it was, it had worked. The next day I got a letter asking me to come by Commander Loran's office in a few days so I could discuss "potentials for future consultation work" with him. It was presented as optional, but it was clear that if I said no I'd need to flee the country. It was also exactly what I was looking for. Before I could get in there, though, I needed to tell a certain spy about it to see what I needed to look out for.

CHAPTER 19

✶

A FRANK CONVERSATION

People gave me confused looks as I entered the military building, but I had a letter, inviting me to come and meet with the commander at a specified hour. It was clear that I was supposed to be here, so I was let in and brought to a waiting area while people came and went all about me.

"Ah, good to see you; please come in," Commander Loran said as he opened his door, the smile on his face wide. "Sit, sit. Would you like some tea?"

"Please," I said. Tea was a commonality among the elves, too, largely because His Majesty had been known to be very fond of it, keeping his own gardens for growing his preferred blends.

"Thank you," I said as I took the glass, a pleasantly sweet, floral scent wafting from it.

"Young man, you know, I'm so glad to see you, to talk to you today." He pushed a small crystal on his desk, and I felt the magic buzz into existence at the edges of the room. "Privacy ward," he said. "Standard issue for any talks that might be sensitive."

"And you think this talk will be sensitive?" I asked. We'd only met the one time.

"Of course," he remarked. "I am dealing with a spy from a, well, not hostile nation, but one we're certainly not friends with."

My blood went cold, and training took over. I stopped the cup where it was, halfway to my lips.

"But don't worry," he reassured me. "If I'd wanted you dead or arrested, I would have done so already." He motioned to my tea. "Please drink up; it's not poisoned."

"What makes you think I'm a spy?" I asked, trying to sound confused.

"Your contacts. The young lady. We've been watching her for some time now. Again, though, she's from Atal, not a hostile state, not even a particularly antagonistic one. I figured she was just a watcher, so I was happy to let her be. You never know what you might find out."

"I'm not sure . . ."

"I've not insulted your intelligence, Percival. Please do not insult mine. What I'm concerned about is why you're here. Neither nation has any particular issue with ours, so far as I'm aware; nor are you trying to acquire military technology."

"No particular issue?" I asked.

"Well, certainly there is always some low-level competition between neighbors, but we've not had a war with Atal for . . . goodness, almost a thousand years. As far as human nations go, longer than that. While I know that many of my comrades dislike humanity, and even more dislike humans in our nation, or those with their blood, it does seem a bit premature for them to send someone to spy on us. If we were going to attack, it would be obvious."

"Certainly you can understand the concern?" I asked. "With how you treat those with less elvish blood, how would you treat humans?" I asked.

"It's . . . complicated, quite complicated. The issue with those of thin blood isn't hatred, though I'm sure it seems that way. Did you know that the less elven blood one has, the lower our people's propensity for magic? Only a few hundred years ago, nearly every elf had magic, but now, we're seeing more and more people crossbreeding with humans, and as they do, fewer and fewer become mages."

"We live with few mages," I observed.

"Yes, you do, but our whole society runs on magic. The idea was to introduce human blood because you're far more fecund than us, but . . . but it's not working. In groups without true ancients that can add an infusion of their own blood now and then, we're slowly weakening, faster than the birth rates rise. If it were to continue, then we'd surely collapse. I've seen the estimates—whole cities would cease to function."

"Surely you could survive," I told him. "We do."

"Our magical beasts are both far more common and far more vicious than those in human lands, young man. I know it seems odd, but there are creatures here that threaten entire cities. Having the mana to establish proper shields isn't an option. Without them they will suffer greatly. And so . . . we've taken to encouraging people toward purity. Yes, it is unfortunate. Yes, some suffer, but surely you see the logic?"

I considered for a while, really thinking through what he was saying. I believed there were ways around it, surely, but did he? He really might not, and I had to admit, I'd never seen the monsters he spoke of. Without technology to fill the gap, there might be great destruction.

"I do," I finally said. "I believe your methods are wrong, but I see the logic. There are reasons for what you've done on that account. Perhaps I would have taken a different route, but the ways of governments are not always the same as that of men. Their concerns are different. However, it has gone beyond encouragement. I met a girl recently who was outright abused, afraid to so much as speak, afraid to stand up for herself. Her employer even offered her to me. What do you have to say about that?" I asked.

At this, his lip curled back in disgust. It was not a trained reaction, and from what I could tell, a true one.

"That is highly illegal," he said. "Please tell me who this individual is so that they might be punished."

"The hotel I'm staying at," I informed him. "But similarly, the goblins. I know what happened to their island. How was that needed?" I asked.

"The . . . Those green beasts? Goodness, surely you wouldn't defend them?! They're monstrous creatures, destroyers! Our own records tell us this, as well as the fact that they destroyed your city, or parts of it. It was in the news a while back. We heard how they overran it, killed hundreds, destroyed whole districts. Why in the world does our aggression against them bother you?"

"Perhaps your records were mistaken, or perhaps they've changed. I've known a few of them, spoken to them. They're young, and were misled, but a number of them split from the group that attacked our city, even provided some small aid against their fellows."

"I doubt our records were incorrect. From my understanding, they are records of stories His Majesty himself told to the people—records of a great warrior who slew small green creatures; a silent, stoic man who, with his group of friends, tracked them wherever he could, slaying them without mercy."

"Where is this record? I've never heard about it."

"It's a rather obscure text, and not one widely distributed, since it's mostly stories for children. There are some nuggets of wisdom, but those are generally better described by other stories. It is clear, though, that goblins are rapey, vicious monsters, unambiguously."

"Maybe they were at some point, but the ones I've met are quite polite. Well, some of them; others were rather destructive. Regardless, where do we go from here? I assume your men are going to come in here and arrest me or something." That had been the assumption as soon as he'd accused me of being a spy, as was the idea that I was already surrounded, probably from the moment I'd stepped in this room.

"Hmm? No, not presently. I could arrest you, and I could hand you over to others who would probably kill and torture you for information, but I think that's counterproductive at this moment."

I blinked, honestly surprised.

"Instead, I have a proposal for you."

CHAPTER 20

AN OFFER

"A proposal? What kind of proposal?" I asked Commander Loran.

"I want you to do as you were bid."

"What?" I asked.

"I want you to investigate our lands, our people, our home, and I want you to return and tell your leaders that we're no issue at all, because we aren't."

"Sorry, I'm not following." And I really wasn't.

"Well, I'd like to hear what you have to say, in a general sense, and there will be some places that you won't be able to go, of course. Technology and other things that are secure can't be shared, naturally."

"I'm uninterested in your technology. Some of it is very good, don't get me wrong, but we couldn't remake it even if we tried. It is too magic intensive." That comment got me a raised eyebrow.

"Really?"

"It's not that it isn't good. It's that we don't have the setup for most of it. The majority of what your people use would be restricted to only noble residences, and would be considered wasteful, even there. The simple fact is that we don't use things like elevators because the amount of mana simply wouldn't be sustainable. Our building specifications are just too different; although some of the safety measures on your . . ." I knew they loved the safety measures on their elevators. One of the guides had gushed over them for almost an hour.

"Some of that might be fine; it's not military technology." He gave me a very strange look. "That's right! You've been reading those books, haven't you?"

I smiled in response. "You really are convinced I won't find anything that would concern my people, aren't you?" I asked him.

"I am, since as far as I've ever heard, we have too many of our own problems to worry about Hediza. The simple fact of it is that I spend most of my time dealing with internal issues and tech. While this may be an investigation looking for hostility, I think it is instead a good opportunity for discussion of an alliance."

"Mind if I say that I'm still worried about some of the things I've seen, mostly regarding the folks you call *thin*? I understand your explanation, but the results on the ground are still . . . concerning."

He leaned back. "I'll admit that I've seen it, too, but I have faith that while there may be a few bad apples, most of my people are good. If you find anything you feel the need to bring to my attention, you're welcome to."

Good or bad, I knew I couldn't convince him of the real issue. Human or elf, it didn't seem to matter—our psychology was very similar. People wanted someone they could blame. It had been this way in every single society I'd ever heard of. There was always some kind of scapegoat, someone other than themselves who they would deem responsible for their problems.

Of course, as soon as they identified this person or entity, violence against them became justified. This pattern had repeated itself through the history of Earth for generations. Here, though, there were much fewer people with human blood, and they tended to have less magic than their fellows. It meant that they may well be doomed unless someone saw reason, like when societies from Earth met more advanced ones and realized they were all one people—well, almost.

"I will," I assured him, though it was only a half-truth.

"I don't suppose you'll tell me why the Atali people are investigating our homeland?" he asked.

"You'll need to ask them. Though, you are on the same continent, so if they think there's a problem, they can handle it themselves. Can you honestly tell me your people aren't spying on *them*?"

"A fair point; though, that's not my department."

"What is?"

"I deal primarily with internal issues stemming from external sources, hence my meeting with you."

That made a simple sort of sense. Every department would get more and more specific, and no doubt there were more specialized departments below his own.

"Well, what do we do first?" I asked.

He laid out a number of places I was now approved to go. They would get me closer to different parts of the government without putting me at risk; though I had no doubt they were all innocuous. There was no reason for him to show me problems. He didn't know what I was looking for, though, and that was all the better for me.

While I looked through the documents he provided, knowing it was all propaganda, I thought back. I needed to alert my contact that she'd been burned. Even if she wasn't one of my people, I owed her that much. Surely he knew that, and if he hadn't picked her up already, he would probably let her go. There were ways to let people know that an operation was compromised. I'd have to do it, and it would suck, but it had to be done.

I was allowed to leave the office, and I was grateful. There'd been no promise of that when I came in, and less of one once it became clear he knew I was a spy. At least some of the reasoning was still quiet though. I still needed to see if I could find out who or why anyone would have had our archmage killed. Perhaps that wasn't Commander Loran's department, but it was someone's, and when I found them, the full might of several very old, very powerful people would be coming down upon them.

CHAPTER 21

✶

KARMA

There were things I needed to do upon getting back to my room. The first was simple enough. Tea. There was a pot and plenty of water in my room, so making it was no problem at all. The blend I had was smooth, light, and somewhat fruity. Perfect.

I sat down with my tea by the window—fully open to the sky—and began reading. The natural light streamed over the papers, so that I could examine each in detail, looking for issues and for what I was after, information.

An open window was also the signal that we'd all been burned, giving my co-conspirator a chance to know she'd been made. I had to at least try to help her.

As for the information itself, it was primarily propaganda, which was to be expected, but that didn't mean it wouldn't be helpful. Commander Loran thought I was after information on invasions, on large attack plans and military information, and sure, I would love to see that, but that wasn't all. I wanted more than that, information on who sent people to my city. Sadly, he didn't have that.

What he did have, and hadn't realized he'd given me, was access to cultural information. Not state secrets, but programs that were made for getting to them. The people who'd come to my home had been elves, yes, but they'd been disguised. They were elves with altered ears and a near-perfect command of our language. Spies.

So I began to look for where the spies might be, where they might be coming from. There were few places in this land that taught human languages, and fewer still that taught my native tongue, much less well enough to fool locals. So that's where I'd begin, because certainly someone in those programs would be connected.

Then I would need to find out who was doing the surgeries to alter their ears. That meant government and medical. A priest, perhaps, since they worked by different standards here than the Orders. The Orders of Hediza wouldn't have allowed one of their members to do such a thing, but they had very little power on Elazia. No, it was a much more patchwork system, but it worked for them.

In my homeland, every priest was part of the Orders. I suspected that they might kill or detain those who tried to avoid them, and for good reason. Why? Well, I'd already seen one rogue priest, and nobody wanted even a weak one around. They were too deadly, so children were taken to them when they displayed power. It was an open secret that those who didn't get with the program often died mysteriously; though that was very, very rare. Priests, after all, seemed to have a sort of built-in moral compass, and they just needed somewhere to fit in.

Here, though, it was different. The Orders were around, to a very limited extent, but it seemed they were intentionally kept weak. No child was ever handed over to them. Instead, children were educated mostly by the state. There were schools and classes, some of which were at the colleges I'd visited, and listed in the information before me now. I needed to go and observe some of those classes and find the likely culprits responsible for infiltrating my homeland.

So, with the information Commander Loran had given me, along with the access, mixed with what the universities had shown me, I began to filter out my options. Was this program likely to have anyone who could do what I'd seen? No? Then I could put it to the side. Was that elf good enough at linguistics? No, certainly not, not enough to fool a native speaker. One program might have managed, but they had a human teacher, a rarity here, and that whole school was run by a slightly anti-government administration. I still needed to check them, but they were almost off the list.

Some of the different priestly groups too. They were all very open about what they believed. Many just didn't feel right, though. Their ideals would clash with spy-making. Some were almost like government agencies themselves, and those I would need to look at. Then, there were a few independent priests, and if there was even one . . . Well, I wasn't sure how to deal with that.

The day waxed and waned. I'd gotten back from my meeting fairly early, all things considered, and began this project shortly thereafter. As evening approached there was a light, hesitant knock on my door.

I rose, crossing the room and opening it to find the maid who'd been serving me for most of my time here, behind her a small cart with food on it.

"Please forgive the interruption, but normal dinner service is closed. There has been an . . . issue with some of the staff, and it is causing a bit of a disruption to our dining facilities, so we've been instructed to bring evening meals to our guests instead," she explained.

With an owlish blink, I looked at the window. The sun was sinking low already, just now starting to go to the horizon.

"Oh, goodness, look at the time," I replied, having completely lost track of it. "One moment, please."

I gathered up my stacks of paper, putting them aside for the moment and clearing the small table in the room before motioning her in.

She moved with efficiency, bringing over the food.

"If it's not too much to ask, what happened?" I inquired.

"There was some issue with some of the senior staff. Some government regulators showed up and, apparently, found evidence of some wrongdoing. I am unfamiliar with the details, sir, but please rest assured that we're handling it as best we can. Please rest assured that we will minimize the impact on your stay."

I wanted to laugh. I had some idea as to what they'd been here about, and why it was the senior staff who were in trouble. Well, Commander Loran had at least earned a little bit of goodwill from me. Even if the rest of it were rotten, he at least kept his word on one account.

One by one, she sat out dishes—local fish, more fruits I didn't recognize, a full pot of some juice or other that looked blue. It all smelled lovely, at least.

"You're looking at schools?" she said, seeing the pile of papers, and indeed, most of what I was looking at were schools.

"Yes, though I know very little about them individually."

"Oh . . . forgive my curiosity, sir, but you may want to consider going to a different one," she said, indicating the one on the top of my pile. It had a good linguistics program, but wasn't really one of the top contenders, from what I was seeing.

"Why's that?" I asked.

"Well, they don't take . . . people with much human blood, and they might be a bit unfriendly to you," she said, hesitant.

"Is that so?" I inquired. "Their information doesn't say such things."

"Ah . . . well, yes, if you're not used to looking at it, but there are a few keywords, things everyone puts in their public documents to show how much they support the anti-human movement."

I wanted to laugh. That was the sort of thing I wouldn't know, that I would struggle to find out, but a local, particularly one with a lot of human blood, had to know. She had to know what places to avoid if she didn't want to endure the racism and negative interactions, the dangers to her personally.

"Why, thank you for telling me that. If you don't mind, could you please elaborate, or tell me which of these is like that, and how you know?"

"Um . . . Yes sir, that should be no problem," she said, clearly happy to help someone who'd been nice to her before, even if she was a bit nervous in general.

A smile crossed my face, for a good deed had done me right today. Had Commander Loran not been informed of their offenses against this girl, and had he not acted on it, she wouldn't be here, wouldn't see those papers, and I might have missed a critical piece of information. Karma was surely a bitch for somebody, but she was being nice to me today.

As I turned back, I saw it, a candle lit in the window of a room across the way—the return signal that my message had been received, and another load off my back.

CHAPTER 22

★

CHECKING CAMPUSES

My maid had given me excellent, well-thought-out advice, designed to keep me out of trouble. I promptly ignored it. My goal was to find who was in charge of causing these problems so they might be removed with prejudice. I didn't know what the thousands-of-years-old elf who'd lost a good friend was planning, but I was guessing that it would be very final.

To that end, I began looking over the places I could go that were the most aggressive to people with human blood. They could only do so much, as I was there with explicit military permission, but at the same time, I expected to see something if I looked deeply enough. It was a simple enough matter, and so I arranged things, starting with the places that seemed most unpleasant to me, given what the maid had said.

The first was a college campus, and as soon as I arrived, I noticed some of the differences. It was subtle, but each and every one of the people here had at least one ear exposed, and all of their ears were far longer than those of the average citizen. Some were even decorated with multiple earrings, not an uncommon thing, in general, but it was much more obvious.

"Greetings," the man tasked with showing me around said; though, it sounded like he wanted to puke when he said it. "I understand you have requested to visit our esteemed institute. I thank you for your interest. Please allow me to show you around our grounds."

The grounds were beautiful. I got looks, a lot of looks, and my guide was constantly going on about how this was one of the most ancient and revered learning institutes in the region; their programs only accepted the best. It was like hearing someone going on about an ivy league school, if the school came off as exceedingly racist at first glance.

"I understand you have a quality linguistics program?" I asked after looking around their design and magical tech labs for a while. They were fancy, but the students weren't doing anything spectacular.

"Of course, of course," he said. "We have programs for all sensible disciplines. Would you like to see it?"

"Certainly. I've seen so few in my time here, and it would do to see the best." It was not the best at all, and I well knew it, but it was the one that hated humans the most.

"Wonderful, then I shall be happy to enlighten you." I didn't miss the barb.

Their complex was indeed impressive, a large building built around an ancient tree, which looked to have been grown into its shape. However, what I found inside was . . . lackluster. They mostly studied dialects of elven languages, and at those they were quite skilled. However, when it came to human languages the professors themselves seemed barely fluent, their accents so thick that their students would have had trouble if they ever ended up where I was from.

We spent a long time there, and after seeing that they couldn't properly conjugate a verb in my mother tongue, I knew that this, at least, wasn't where my enemies had come from. Of course, that didn't change anything. I still had to sit through the full lecture—I had asked to see the place, after all—and hear the man, whose name I couldn't remember and didn't care to, speak down to me about their facilities.

"I assume you learned from your family? Your pronunciation of our own language is quite nearly proper," he said.

"No, actually, my family is from a different region. An older kindly elf decided generously to instruct me on your dialect."

"Oh, how wonderful; though I'm sure your childhood experience helped. You can always tell when someone learned when they were older," he said with a wink.

"What was the giveaway?" I asked, though he was full of it. I'd actually learned recently.

"Several of your vowels, for example . . ." He gave a really rather long explanation about verbal stops and mouth position that I hadn't actually mastered yet, but it was good information to have; it might help me later.

Eventually, I did get free from the disaster I'd brought upon myself, and began to plan my next visit to another school.

The ear thing was something I'd missed, and the maid hadn't let me in on it. Perhaps it was obvious to her, or had slipped her mind. Many things that we took for granted as normal weren't obvious to people from other cultures. Now that I saw it though . . .

Nearly everywhere I looked I started seeing it, ears visible on men or women who might have otherwise hidden them beneath hair, and always at least one visible. On others, particularly those who seemed to be in lower status jobs, not always. It also gave me ideas of good places to look, paintings and advertising people, watching who they went for and who they ignored. It was a good measure one could see at a glance, as my ears were less pointed than my mother's, whose were less pointed than her father's.

Regardless, with my first option down, I began to look at other potential locations where I might find our enemies. The next two places on my list were much like the first, though one of them was notably more hostile. I wasn't asked to leave, but their explanations were so brief that it was clear they wanted me to.

By the time I got to the fourth school on my list, I had all but given up. The people here were condescending, but they were at least polite, and their language class was . . . well, actually it was pretty good. I saw people conversing in the dialect most common in norther Hediza, and their accents weren't even too thick. The teacher didn't have one at all.

"Would you care to speak with us a bit?" the professor asked me. "I find it may be useful for my students to speak with a native. My own patterns of speech are limited, sadly."

He was right. His tone was a mixture of academia and . . . well common. There were inflections, tells that my own mother and grandma had been very particular about during my youth. Think of the word *bath* and how one might pronounce it differently depending on what part of the country they're from.

"Certainly," I agreed.

The following hour wasn't particularly productive, as we spoke about very plain subjects, but we did drift a bit here and there, speaking of our favorite locations.

"I've never gotten to see a pine forest," one of the girls said.

"I hear there are several in the north," another added.

"They're quite lovely. The way they smell is my favorite thing about them, and when the wood is being processed, it fills the air with magnificent scents. Though, the pollen from pine trees can be a bit much," I told them.

Our conversation drifted, and the students were happy to have someone they could practice with who wasn't a professor or fellow student, and most were quite polite, if nothing else. Though, a few were a bit standoffish.

In fact, this discourse went so late that the sun was going down when I left. The healing hall was nearby, a short walk away, and as I passed it, I saw a man leaving with his ears covered, a thick hat pulled down over them. That wasn't news to me, but he stood out, even with his uniform that designated him as part of the armed forces. It was probably the only reason he wasn't being stared at by the students.

CHAPTER 23

★

SPY WORK

How interesting, I thought as I followed the man at a distance. Sure, I stood out, but he did, too, and I had exceptional senses. Moreover, while he was military, I'd been trained to join our own military. Sure, much of that had been combat training, but moving unobserved was part of combat. I had a feeling this man didn't share a physical aspect, at least, if for no other reason than how he moved. We had a way when we got stronger, a certain . . . step, a method of moving around people, past people, for you had to be careful because your muscles had more power in them than others.

My target had none of that, and as he moved, I did too. He slipped through alleys, and I slipped over, the darkness helping. It wouldn't help me against a prepared and trained man, but for now, I just looked like a young physical magic user trying to avoid the streets, keeping an eye in shop windows as I zigzagged behind him.

I was expecting him to go to the main military headquarters, or perhaps the residential section of town. That would have made sense but, alas, he did not. Instead, he headed toward the docks. That was unfortunate, because as we got nearer, I saw him heading for a pier, and that was too far for me to follow. I could see guards down there, and while it looked like I was just passing now, if I lingered, it would not, and getting caught was no good at all. I had to abandon my mission, roaming north along the lake edge, as there truly was a massive lake. It looked like a small sea.

I moved back toward the city proper, back toward where I was staying, back to the safe areas. I wondered if Commander Loran knew of this, but asking would keep me from doing what I'd come here to do, from learning what I needed to learn.

That in mind, I returned to my room. A quick check confirmed that a certain light was out, meaning I was alone for now. That was a true shame, but one that I knew could happen. It was better for my allies not to get caught than be there only to make me feel better. This was my mission.

The following day I did as I had been doing—another college I'd managed to get an invite to, another place where the elves would be rude and condescending. They had no language program of note when it came to human dialects, so there was no evidence there. Much to everyone's pleasure, though, I cut that visit shorter than previous ones. The interviewees were almost as happy to see me go as I was to leave them.

I was back in my room before sunset, and I had finished changing my clothes right as the sun dipped behind the buildings. I slipped out of my room, the loose, easy-to-move-in outfit hanging around me. Now, some people think that a ninja should be wearing black, that it's the color to wear to hide in shadows. Those people are stupid. The fact of the matter is that it depends on where you are, but a mix of dark greens, blues, and browns is much, much better for hiding at night.

The second important thing is to break up the lines of your face. People are really good at seeing faces, like scary good, even in the dark, even hidden. Facial lines stick out like a sore thumb. A lump you might ignore, but a lump with a face? You'd see that a mile away.

So, with that in mind, I set off. I had a few small things to help me should I get in trouble, and something I could pull over myself to make me look like an elven man out for a walk. It was different, seeing things as I was. In the time I'd been here, I had mostly been seen as a rich foreigner, but from the ground . . .

People sneered at me, actually sneered at me. Everywhere I moved through the city, my outfit just good enough to look reasonably like something a local would wear, they made faces and upturned their noses. They seemed . . . unhappy. It was odd, a very new experience, and I didn't much like it at all. Seeing this sort of prejudice from the other side really was something.

"Get out of my way," a man said, pushing past me. I could have easily dropped him, but attention wasn't what I wanted, so I moved.

It was like this everywhere. Some of the business owners nearby made it clear I wasn't welcome, even when it was clear I wasn't heading toward their businesses. Women sneered, men frowned. Everywhere I went it was the same. Honestly, it was depressing. Did the maid from my hotel get this same reaction? Perhaps for her it was worse. She had to live it daily, after all, and unlike her, nobody was looking at me in an inappropriate way.

So, I hurried along, making my way toward the college. This city had a number of them, mostly smaller institutions resting around the edges, but still, a really surprising number of higher educational institutions for this place.

Before I got there, because there was no way they were going to let me through the gate, I hid, covering my head and face and moving into the shadows. My training had mostly been about fighting, but stealth was an important part of that sometimes.

This university didn't have great security. It had some, sure, but there was only so much you could do when your school was in the middle of a city with people coming and going all day long, unless you wanted an innumerable flood of false alarms. They apparently did not, so getting onto the campus had been easy enough.

I was also lucky that this particular place catered more to the thinking class, rather than those like me who had enhanced physical capabilities. I quietly made my way through the night, listening for footsteps and avoiding people as best I could, hiding in the shadows. I neared the building a man in a hat had come out of.

It was easier than I'd feared, harder than I'd hoped, and actually kind of fun. There were plenty of bushes, plenty of places nearby to sit. Perhaps I could have gotten closer had I merely walked up at one point during the day, but my hope was that by coming at night I could get inside once the staff and students had cleared out for the night.

On that account I was partially successful, for the staff and students had indeed left, but there were still people inside. I could tell. I saw some evidence of protections on the doors and windows; though they hadn't warded the whole building. My strongest sense was my hearing, something I'd used to navigate the world around me since I was little. Even now, I could hear a handful of people inside, moving about.

Two men, if I had to guess by the cadence and weight of their steps, moved through a hall near to one another, unspeaking. As they turned a corner a woman responded to them.

"Ah, everything well, doctors?" she asked.

"Yes, just checking on our patient," one of them called back to her. "Any news?" one of them called back to her.

"Reports say he's well," the woman replied. "Though, last I spoke to him, he was very unhappy."

They entered a room where someone was pacing. Bare feet on stone was a bit harder to read, but based on context, I was guessing another man.

"Have things settled?" one of the doctors asked him.

"Yes, though it disgusts me," the patient responded. "Why must we go through this?"

"You know the answer, and we've lost good men already. We need our replacements, or else our plans will be very limited."

"Fine, you're right. We must do what is needed, for the glory of our people," the patient said, to noises of approval.

CHAPTER 24

✶

TRUTH OF THE MATTER

"Very well," the patient said after some time. "Tell me what I must do."

"Heal first," the doctor said. "Your commander will have your orders when you get to him. My brother, Oras, I know that this shames you, this . . . horrid thing we've done, but things are changing, and we must act. Word has reached me recently that the humans may even be working with the goblins."

"Surely not? Even if they're misled, they can't be *that* misled," the patient, clearly Oras, responded.

"They don't have access to the old books we do. They don't know the monsters they bed with. Regardless, it complicates things. We cannot and must not allow them to support one another. The green barbarians are said to breed fast, and with access to human women . . ."

Well, that didn't make sense at all. Back on Earth there'd been many stories of goblins being quite, well, rapey, but here? No, from my understanding of it, they had a completely different genome, one incompatible with ours. Both Sasha and one of the human priests had already confirmed it.

"Filth the humans may be, but not even they deserve that fate. It seems we must save the misguided fools from themselves," the doctor said. "Once we rule over them again, we'll set things right, make sure to clean up the green menace once and for all. You'll help in that regard, Oras, though I've not been told specifically what you'll be doing."

I'd really have loved for them to spill more details, but that wasn't how things worked. While these people decidedly knew some of what was going on, they didn't know all of it, and they didn't know this man's mission. Perhaps they knew he was being sent to our lands. Perhaps they knew he had something to do with the goblins. They were even telling him now. But specifics? No, that would wait until he needed to know.

Sighing would be nice, but it was important for me to stay quiet. There were tricks to moving around other people with super senses, and one of them was being as quiet as possible. There were others with hearing like mine, some even more developed, and it wouldn't do to be found out. There were even tricks to walking, making sure you didn't make noise when you did it—staying low, staying quiet, and being extra careful. Even that wasn't foolproof, but it was good enough.

I now had what I needed. Sure, I didn't have all the information, but I knew where the people were coming from. With that alone there would be enough proof that . . . well, they were sending people to our lands. Sadly, I didn't know who exactly was responsible, but these people were at least partially involved, and I had a feeling that when one or two of the older mages showed up, they'd piss themselves before spilling everything. The two I knew scared me, and we were on the same side.

That was enough. Now that my mission was complete, it was time to call in the heavy hitters. So, I retreated, slowly, carefully, back the way I'd come. Once I was off the campus I took to the roofs again, slinking through the night like a shadow. It wasn't the correct way to move through the city, but it was fast.

Once I got back to my room I pulled the curtains right way, with lamp angled so that anyone watching might see. I didn't know how long it would take for anyone to notice, or how many watchers there were, nor even how long until I would be extracted. The message to my handlers was simple and clear: I found where they're coming from.

Of course that didn't mean I was done. Until I was extracted I still had to look like I was being a good watcher. There were still a few more colleges on my list to check out, even if I knew they weren't guilty of this particular crime. Mostly, it was just for show.

I also had another meeting with Commander Loran, for what that was worth. He asked me to join him two days after I'd found out about the infiltration to my homeland.

"Greetings," the commander said. "I do hope you were satisfied by what you found."

"Not satisfied really, but I can't honestly say that's what I was here for."

"Well, satisfied that I'm not actually lying about not having any real animosity to your people."

I actually laughed at that. "Well, no, but I think you don't intend to harm us, at least," I told him, meaning only him. "Honestly, your people really don't like humans."

"Please relate that to your leaders when you return."

"I will, though I'm not scheduled to leave for a while yet," I told him. "Any suggestions on other places to visit? Your recommendation on the universities was quite good."

"More like them or something a bit more relaxed?"

"While I quite enjoyed seeing your technology, something cultural perhaps?" I asked, ready to be gone from here, and not really looking forward to being talked down to any more.

"Several ideas on that one." He provided me with a short, handwritten list of things I might enjoy, which I read over and pocketed.

After my brief meeting with the commander, I returned to my accommodations. We'd begun late, so it was dark now, the sun long set behind the buildings. My feet slapped the cobbles, the many long, smoothed stones brushing against the bottoms of them in a way that almost reminded me of home.

As I turned the corner, I saw it—the maid, my maid, being dragged out by two soldiers.

"Wait, wait, no I've got all my authorizations," she pleaded with them.

"In with you," one of the guards said, hauling her into a cart and following along behind her. He was rough, brutal, as he hauled her in, and my heart hurt; though it also raged.

She'd helped me, and I couldn't help her. There were witnesses, many witnesses. Several of the staff. This maid, this woman, had been instrumental in my mission, to my success, and now she suffered. It brought back memories of all the stories of people my former nation had failed—men who'd been abandoned by soldiers sworn to protect them. I'd made no such promise to her, no agreement, no contract, even verbally. Regardless, I could not, and would not, abandon her. I had to live with myself.

As the cart began to slip away, the back closed and sealed, I slipped back into the shadows, following the cart as close as I dared.

CHAPTER 25

✶

STOLEN AWAY

There were choices, two of them. First, and properly, the most legal one, was to go to Commander Loran and ask for his help. He might help me. He might even help this girl, if I requested it. However, I had a feeling that this wasn't his doing in the first place, nor his area of expertise. The fear in her voice, the panic I saw in her as they loaded her into the cart told me that something was deeply wrong, something I didn't yet understand. For now, I would follow and see where they were taking her, so that I could get him to release her. Or, if that seemed unlikely, I would take option two—rescue her myself.

One problem was that following like this was slightly risky. There were a lot more mages here than in my own homeland, with nearly everyone having at least a minor talent. Most of the lesser mages were weak, but there were still quite a few of them. It was one of the things the elves prided themselves on—their sheer number of magic users.

It hadn't stopped me before, of course; though, before I'd mostly been moving from place to place, and that could easily be explained. This time, I was following someone, which was less simple to explain as being rude while traveling, more so because they were clearly authorities, and most people understood that there really were only so many reasons to follow a cop car.

And if I had to fight? Well, I had a few weapons on me—a pistol, of course; some knives; no long blade, like I generally used, but I was armed. I'd not been prepping for war tonight, so what I could bring to bear was limited by design. I was still fast and strong, faster and stronger than even an average physical magic user, though by no means faster and stronger than some. Nor was I a monster, who could bowl through dozens like they were made of paper.

It took longer than I'd hoped for them to reach their destination. By the time we got there, I was sweating, worried that I might have to follow them for hours and hours. It appeared to be a government building, a police station or something, perhaps? No, smaller than any of the major ones, but they pulled a few people from the back of the car.

That was good. They were just bringing her and some others to the station . . . Wait. They weren't taking them inside. Rather than heading for the front door, where one would expect to see prisoners taken, or even to a side door, they headed around the back. Something seemed . . . wrong about this. They weren't heading for any of the doors at all, and the prisoners they had—all of whom were clearly of less elven blood—were beginning to get more agitated. Several were calling out to the guards, asking them to merely allow them to go and get their proper identifications, but the guards seemed not to care.

They were being taken to trains. From what I could see, they looked like normal passenger line trains, but a train nonetheless, out of the city. Every hair on the back of my neck stood up as I watched people board the train, one after another. The windows were small, and my vision wasn't perfect for this sort of distance, but from where

I was, I could see that they were putting the prisoners in seats, ostensibly with handcuffs. Their faces looked out the small windows, and I moved.

I couldn't see where they were going, and I certainly couldn't get onboard one of those train cars, or rescue the girl here. There were too many witnesses, too many guards, but I could figure out what they were doing. So, I got ahead of the vehicle, crouched low, and moved along the line. It was clear what direction the train was going, so making my way down the tracks half a mile or so caused me no issues. I hid there, high in a tree.

It was nearly an hour before I saw the train pass, half a dozen cars full of scared-looking elves. As it reached the end, I leapt from my hiding spot and landed with a soft thud on the final car. The time to find out some more truths had arrived.

Chien

"Yes, sir, we saw the sign yesterday, but he isn't there," the agent said through the receiver, and something on the back of my neck tickled.

"Explain," I said. "What do you mean isn't there? Was he taken?"

"I don't think so, sir. It doesn't look like his room has been disturbed more than one would expect for standard cleaning. He's just not been seen all day."

"His last known location?"

"Reports indicated investigation of several colleges, though no information on what he found, and a potential relationship with a local commander by the name of Loran."

I had files on him and had read them. I had no need to do so again. "He's in charge of internal matters, though not overly associated with the politics, unless something has changed recently . . . I'm sending down a few trackers. Find the lad. He clearly has information we want, and I believe he might be important."

In truth, he was, at least, mildly important. The boss liked people like him, people with that strange aura, people who spoke that odd language of his. They were all connected, and for the most part, seemed to genuinely want to do good. I did not want to be the one to tell him that we'd lost the boy.

So, instead I got up, moved through the building, sending out orders, and was shortly met with a small team before a teleport gate, one the boss himself had made for us.

"We're going through. We're after a human named Percival. You should all have received the information."

They all saluted. In my hand, I held a small, sealed jar with one of the boy's socks, something I'd snagged on our voyage to Elazia. These men weren't fighters. They were trackers, each with specialized senses, as well as few support staff healers and mages. They weren't muscle, and they wouldn't need it. I was going with them. If the southerners had decided to get restive and take that boy, I'd be retrieving him myself, or else the boss might, and nobody wanted that.

CHAPTER 26

FACILITY

It was not a short trip. There were guards on the train, armed ones; though, I had a feeling they were rather poorly trained, but people who weren't the best or brightest that had been tasked with guarding these people. Perhaps they thought that the more thinly blooded elves were inconsequential. Perhaps they just didn't care. Perhaps they were right. The prisoners weren't fighting.

That struck a chord in me. Too many times governments had been abusive and their people hadn't fought back. They had allowed themselves to be led to the slaughter like lambs. The Nazis had done it, the Communists had done it. Every oppressive government had gathered up and murdered people en masse, and they hadn't fought. It hurt me to see that these people were being held against their will, but I didn't know if they were being harmed beyond that just yet.

There was still crying coming from the scared people below me. I could hear it. I could hear their words drifting up through the train cars, the guards patrolling, the rattle of the train itself as it traveled down the tracks. Man, the rattle. This thing was poorly built. I carefully made my way to the front, where the engine was, keeping low and out of sight, particularly when I was near others who might see me. The engine on this thing had to be purely magical, as there was no smoke, something I was grateful for, but it sounded . . . off.

I had spent hours over the course of this trip sitting and listening to the sounds of the train, and it struck me. They weren't using magic to turn the wheels, but rather to propel the train forward, much like I did with my aircraft. It worked, sure, but it was also a brute-force solution, a simple one, the one that people used when they weren't optimizing for distance, but for ease. Even if I'd used it myself, I still found it very disappointing that these people, who spent so much time optimizing their magic, used such a . . . blunt method of pushing a train forward.

"How much longer?" I heard one of the soldiers ask one of the conductors below.

"An hour or two at most. Are you sure we're doing the right thing here?" the man responded. "I mean, I've never had a full train come back . . ." That put my teeth on edge.

"We're helping them. They may not like it, and they may suffer, but it's the right thing to do. This helps all of us, fixes this mess others have wrought." There wasn't a moment's hesitation in his voice. "Are you doubting now?"

"No, just . . . there was a kid, and he looked so scared . . ."

"Don't worry, they're just thinnies," the soldier said, using a slang term for elves with very little elven blood.

"Right."

I saw the destination well before I reached it, and abandoned the train. This was achieved by simply jumping off the back and into a nearby ditch.

Oh dear, I thought to myself as I sailed through the air. *I may have miscalculated just a bit.*

In fact I had. I had not bled off nearly enough of the momentum that I had in me. I ended up rolling and sputtering in the dirt. Rocks sailed around me as I hit the ground, and if I'd not been as tough as I was, I probably would have broken at least a few bones. Thankfully, I was a physical magic user, so even if I wasn't specialized for durability, I could take a beating that would kill lesser men.

"Let's see what's what," I said as I rose, dusting myself off as I headed in the direction of the facility.

It wasn't, as I had feared, some kind of death camp, but that's where the good news ended. There were multiple buildings, all quite secure looking, with a large fence around the perimeter, which opened to allow the train in and to disgorge the people aboard it.

A quick run around the border revealed that the facility was roughly star shaped, with nine points. There were a few outdoor areas, and I could see elves, all clearly thin blooded, and all under guard and in some kind of uniform.

They didn't look good. The prisoners were clearly exhausted, scared, and having issues, but they weren't as bad as I might have feared either. None looked to be starving. There were a few children with what looked to be their parents, kept close. There were no outward signs of extreme physical abuse, even if all of them appeared tired and broken mentally.

Clearly, this place was a prison of some form. Though, from my vantage point, there was a very limited amount that I could learn. I could return now and ask for the release of the young woman who'd been so decent to me, but would that help her? Would finding this place change things? Perhaps I could even ask my benefactors to shut it down; they might be able to do that.

Something about those ancient elves I'd met, and the way they'd carried themselves, told me that when they came it was going to be fire and fury, and woe to all who might stand in their way. Those who'd sent the men to Exion, the ones who'd killed the archmage, were right and fucked if I read the situation correctly. What about the others though? I didn't know. That's not what I was here for.

With a deep sigh, I began to back away. I'd tell the councilor who'd sent me, or the old king himself. I'd ask for them to save the girl, tell them she'd helped me. From what I was seeing, there was no real reason to fear for her life immediately, and the two ancients were coming. She might get hurt here, might be afraid, but me trying something would just make things worse. It was best if I backed off, marked this place, and let the heavy hitters do their part.

I rose to turn and leave when I heard it. There was someone behind me. I spun quickly, only to catch something solid and heavy on my nose, hard enough to send me sprawling and my head spinning.

"Told you I saw something," a voice said.

"True enough . . . Wait, look at him. Young, and his ears," a female responded.

"Interesting, now let's go, kid."

I tried to rise, only to catch another blow—clearly the butt of a rifle—to the face once more. Whoever this was, he was faster than me. That was enough to take me from just stumbling to utter darkness.

CHAPTER 27

★

INTERROGATION

I came to and found myself bound and with a monster of a headache. Also, I'm pretty sure I had a broken nose. A quick check, and yes, indeed, a broken nose. That would heal, but goodness, what a mess.

"Ah, you're awake. You know, I'm quite surprised you're alive. Normally, when Ilan hits someone they don't get back up, but you are tougher than average, aren't you?" a voice said, not unkindly.

"Ugh, a bit, where am I?" I asked, still a bit disoriented.

"An interesting question to be sure, but it should be obvious, no?" As I opened my eyes, I saw the speaker, and the room I was in.

It was an elven man, slightly taller than myself and with some of the longest ears I'd yet seen, save the two ancient ones. He was wearing a white robe over what appeared to be a uniform, not a doctor's coat, but something similar. He looked at me with curiosity, a small smile on his face.

As for the room, well, it was clearly an interrogation room. My hands were chained to the table in front of me, the shackles quite thick and of some steel alloy. In time, I might be able to break them, but it wouldn't be soon. Picking them would be easier. Odd thing, though, locks worked very similarly to those back on Earth, and though I was no expert, I did know what the internals of such things looked like.

"Oh, well that bodes poorly," I said as I looked around.

"Indeed," he replied. "Now, could you tell me what exactly you were doing skulking around our facility?"

"Well, since I've been arrested, perhaps I should know the charges first?" I asked, hopefully.

"Oh arrest is such a nasty word. You're . . . being *held*, pending investigation, and I think you know why. We don't really need such deceptions among ourselves, do we?"

"And if I refuse to cooperate, does the niceness stop?" I asked. There weren't any instruments in the room for torture, but that didn't mean there couldn't be.

"Stop? Why would we need to? We're really quite capable of holding you here, willing or not, and . . . Oh, you mean torture. You really aren't from Elazia, are you? I suspected from the accent, but it could have been the north. I'm not too good with those, you see."

I blinked at that. "I did indeed . . ."

"No, that's not helpful. His Majesty said many years ago, and has been proven right time and again, that torture isn't really effective in most situations. Either you can hold out against it, in which case it is useless cruelty, or you cannot, in which case you'll tell us whatever we want to hear, or whatever you think we want to hear, in order to make the pain stop. The counter-methods are also quite simple, and effective as well. Now, if there were some emergency in the moment, and I knew that you knew the answer I needed right that second, perhaps things would be different, but that's hardly the case."

"Well . . . that's reassuring. Sorry, I don't believe I got your name," I said, dropping that line of questioning.

"Ah, I'm Dr. Palan. Nice to meet you, Mr. . . ."

"Percival. No real reason to conceal that, I suppose," I admitted.

"Ah, good. Well, now that we're getting somewhere, why were you here? We do take security quite seriously."

"I'm not even sure where here is, in all honesty. Just following up on something I saw," I said.

"Now, now, let's not be rude."

"That is mostly the truth," I said. "I saw something and decided to investigate. Is that truly an issue?"

"When you follow that something back to a secure facility and spy on us, yes."

"Secure facility? What exactly is it you're doing here, anyway?"

"Holding those of thin blood, and trying to help them as best we can. That isn't a secret, young man. In fact, it's a well-known fact that we're doing so."

I'd heard things, but had never gotten any confirmation on what they were doing *exactly*. I knew that those with little elven blood were . . . well something, but not what. I also hadn't heard about what they were doing to *help* them, an idea which triggered all kinds of alarms.

"Help how?" I asked.

"Ah, well, since you yourself fall into that category, I was hoping you might volunteer to aid us personally. My own tests show that you have roughly five percent elven blood, a really low number to be sure. By our metrics, you're one of the lowest we've yet seen."

"Really? Well, that's interesting, but I'm afraid that I really do have things to do, places to be."

"Do you? With clothes that look like you're a spy, and knives, and really a quite clever little firearm? It's not really my thing, but I'm told that several of our people are quite curious as to where you got it. The design is . . . well, ugly, and a bit in need of some work, but brilliant, I'm told. Did you get it in the north?"

"What an odd question, no? The design is getting more common in Hediza," I informed him. It wasn't a state secret anymore. With more and more officers getting them, I knew for a fact that a few had been leaked.

"A human weapon? Really? I'll admit, I'm surprised, though with the lack of decoration . . . I thought it perhaps a prototype or something."

"Not really, no, and as a point of fact, I've never been to the north, not on your continent."

"Color me surprised. Well then, thank you for letting me know that. Let's get you over to our work area. I have a few tests I'd like to run."

"Did I not say no?"

"Oh, you did. I'm simply choosing to ignore it," he said and pointed at me.

I felt the spell hit and knew what it was supposed to do immediately. It was one I'd been familiar with for a while now. It was supposed to make me go limp, which I did; though, I instinctively resisted the spell itself. There was something to be thankful for when it came to training. That training had sucked, but it might well save me from something now.

"Now, don't worry. We're quite good at what we do here, and I will do all I can to aid you, my young friend. Even if you don't want me to. The administrators have a lot more questions, but those can wait till later, I think. First, we need some baselines."

CHAPTER 28

✶

THE DOCTOR

I was placed in a sort of wheelchair and moved, still limp, though of my own volition. There was no need to tell my enemy that I could fight back. What would be the use in that? No, I needed to play along for the moment and make them comfortable, make them careless. Then I could move.

The metrics were easy. I didn't know where I was. I didn't know the layout. I didn't know what the facility's security was from the inside. Sure, I knew a few things based on what I'd seen from outside, but not enough to ensure that I could escape at the moment. If I got halfway and was caught, things might get far worse.

So, as they wheeled me down the hall, I paid attention. People underestimated how much one could learn from simply observing the world around them. I could see the signs and the halls, and that meant I could get a good understanding of the layout. Sure, I still didn't know where exactly in the facility I was, but I could see that I wasn't underground; I could see the windows as we passed a few. That sounded like a small thing, but seeing where the sun was, knowing if it was going up or down, and the angle compared to what I'd seen before could be of use to me.

My improved memory helped me more here than I'd like to admit. I was on the east side of the facility, assuming I was still in the facility. Given from the images I was seeing through the windows, I was guessing I was. It was at least the second, maybe the third floor, and part of what looked like some kind of medical suite.

While I was pretending to be unable to move, there were some issues. First, my captors weren't stupid, or, at least, they were no fools. Even though they believed me to be helpless, they weren't taking chances. I would not be able to move freely, even should I stop acting, my hands and legs bound to this chair with rather stout looking chains that had small script on them, magical.

Secondly, there were a lot of people here. More than I would've expected, honestly, and I wasn't sure what they could do. Many seemed to be absorbed in their activities, working with various devices, both magical and scientific looking—beakers and the like that they were hovering over, some arguing at what looked like bulletin boards.

"Technically, I don't need to, but I always feel the need to explain what I'm doing to my patients. I hope you don't mind," Doctor Palan, who I was sure was also a priest, began. "Oh, I should allow you to speak, shouldn't I, in case you have questions? Just please remain civil as you have before."

I felt another spell wash over my face and head and turned my eyes to him.

"Is this truly necessary?"

"Yes, now where was I? Oh, yes. Our goal here is to improve the amount of elven blood in our subjects, which is . . . honestly a bit fraught. Part of the issue is that even though we understand well enough how to cast the spells, we're not really sure of the underlying mechanisms. A true issue, no?"

"Indeed," I grunted as he took some blood. Explaining the basics of genetics as I understood them would probably help him, but why would I want to do that.

"For example, sometimes we see odd results, like siblings that are just slightly off from one another. I've yet to find out why. I suspect there's more to it than we know, but . . . well, finding those secrets isn't exactly easy. Why do you think that is? Why do you think there's such variation? Is it some quirk of magic, perhaps? But even those who never touch the power of magic are the same."

"Why should they be the same?" I asked him.

"Well, if they have the same parents, should they not? If I mix red and blue do I not always get purple?"

"People are probably more complicated than that."

"Oh, without a doubt. I'm going to take a bit of blood, not too much, mind, but a bit," he said as he put a needle into my arm, taking . . . really quite a bit of blood.

"That's . . ."

"Not enough to kill you, I assure you, and we do monitor food intake here. I don't want my patients dying; though some do, regardless of what I do to try and save them." He sighed, sounding almost sad, but it didn't stop him. "What we're trying to do here is repair that loss of elven blood, purify people. Honestly, the results have been poor so far, and many of them are injured or having great difficulty being right afterward. Still not sure why."

"Because you're tearing their bodies apart; you have to know that."

"Well, we've been trying to put them back, and we've even had great success with a few, but it seems that sometimes we remove something . . . vital."

It was clear enough to me what they were doing—trying to erase human genes without even understanding genes at all. It was both madness and almost certainly doomed to fail. Missing genes at all was a cause of concern, and erasing whole sections of someone's genome because you didn't know what you were doing? That was murder, and they needed to be stopped.

"Your approach must be wrong, then. You need to understand before acting, or you'll just kill more of your people," I pointed out.

"I . . . have tried to slow things, to do more research—that is true—but my superiors demand results, and should those results be found upon a pile of the dead, well, let us simply say that it is better for me to be here, trying to fix people, rather than someone else who wouldn't care nearly as much. Tell me, since you're from Hediza, do your people have any thoughts or theories that might be helpful?"

"You'd actually consider using human knowledge? And here I thought elves were supposed to be better at everything."

"Posh, I doubt you've got a full explanation for me, but even blind rodents can find food from time to time." That wounded me like a mangled quote about blind squirrels and nuts, but I felt no need to fight it.

"Well, there are a few ideas. It's not really my place of study. For that you'd need a priest, but I have some thoughts. First, explain to me what your current theories are, and I'll see if they match."

"I could complain that I asked first, but it seems pointless. We know that there is some mixing of people when they cross, but that it is extremely complex. Even things like hair and eye color seem to be deeply strange, sometimes even skipping generations before they resurface. Most of this is from records and interviews with some of the elders, who can recall people from their childhoods quite clearly still—their parents and so many people they've met."

"Indeed, it's known to us that hair and eye color seem to be really complex things. I suspect that your issue may be that when you destroy the part of your subjects that is human, you destroy parts like all of the hair or eye coloring, since they don't have any elven colors in them, only human ones. Though, I suppose in that example, it might be something more important than hair color, more like, how the blood should be or something."

"Possible, quite possible, actually, and it would explain some things . . ."

"Maybe you should look at flowers rather than people first. Stop testing things you don't understand, and work with things you do."

"Flowers? Why flowers?"

"I heard a priest had some success breeding them and getting the traits he wanted," I said with a shrug, not willing to do all of the Punnett squares for him, or even tell him what they were. He could spend the time. Better to spare their victims by delaying them, particularly since I was one of those victims at the moment.

"Well, I'm aware there is some breeding with plants, but just growing only the taller ones or ones with pink flowers or . . ."

"No, rumor was he could get the traits the parent plants had, but not the plant in particular, getting them to skip generations or whatnot. Honestly, I never saw the experiments myself, but I did hear the rumors."

"A fascinating idea, but slow. Perhaps I should get some flowers," he said, thoughtfully, as he moved on with shoving a cotton swab up my nose.

CHAPTER 29

✶

IN PRISON

I was floating, and this wasn't accidental. The air held me aloft, suspended in my cell. Some magical setup to keep me in the air above ground, me and the clothing I'd been given. The door, about ten feet out of reach, was thick and sturdy looking, something I would have trouble breaking down, even if it wasn't enchanted. Of course it was. There was a reason people like me were seldom kept as prisoners.

It was really difficult.

They'd also drained enough of my blood and poked at me enough that I was physically exhausted. Just another way to keep me down. The doctors here were priests, of course, which was not great for me, but it did tell me some things, like the fact that they really probably wouldn't torture me or try to cause undue harm. For once, that was working out in my favor.

I would need to act soon, though, and that would bring them upon me. Soon, because this place was madness, and also because if they kept this up, I would slowly weaken. Not this moment, though, since I wasn't sure I had a plan to get out of the floating trap in the center of my room. So, for the moment I listened, trying to hear what I could.

Honestly, it wasn't much. Whoever had designed this place was used to people with magic. It was probably mostly talents, those who had little magic, nearly every elf. That meant they'd been quite thorough, but again, dealing with them and dealing with someone like me wasn't the same thing.

See, there was something the peoples of this world did, something that I considered a flaw, and one I suspected was worse among the elves. They thought in terms of magic and only magic. I'd seen their elevators, and like a lot of them, they were weirdly obsessed. While they had physical stops, most of what was involved was magic, and nearly all of the physics was the same throughout. Now, against normal people, that was smart. Magic was physics-breaking-cheat-levels of power, but it had flaws.

Like the fact that they often ignored parts of physical reality. Lock needs to be better? Enchant it. Door isn't strong enough? Enchant it. Need to hold someone in place? You guessed it—enchantments were the way to go, because obviously they'd use magic to escape. It was a pretty good, pretty accurate policy.

Unless you found someone who didn't try to bash down your door with magic and instead aimed to just . . . take the pins, screws, and fasteners out. Even lock-picking would work pretty well in a lot of places. I'd owned a set of lockpicks back home, and even played around with them a bit. Not that I'd try on this door. After all, there was a difference between playing with padlocks and dealing with an unknown prison door. However, the attachment points were so pretty and vulnerable looking . . .

While I was working through these thoughts, I heard someone approach, knocking.

"Food, then an hour outside. Eat." The man, for it was certainly a male voice, pushed a tray filled with nutritious-looking goop through a small slot and then closed it.

"Huh, how am I supposed to—" I began before gravity returned and I fell to the floor. It wasn't a hard fall, but one far enough for me to catch myself, even if I was disoriented. If I'd not been a physical magic user, that would have been awfully cruel, but I was, and I supposed they knew that.

My afternoon meal was fine, I suppose. Some kind of gruel, almost like a grain, but not quite. Maybe more like a tuber or fruit texture-wise, formed into a slop. It didn't taste bad, per se, but it wasn't good either. It came with a spoon, which I briefly considered stealing, but decided against. It was too obvious. Once I was finished eating, I put the tray back on the little spot by the slot and waited. It took about ten minutes before someone came by.

The guards weren't too concerned about me, for good reason. I may have been strong, but I was a bit off my game, and there were certainly enough of them. I heard the team moving down the halls before I saw them, and when they got to me, they locked me to an actual ball and chain, like in a cartoon. I nearly laughed as I carried the thing down the hallway. It was effective. I wouldn't be able to run or jump, and moving too fast was out of the question. I was strong enough to walk with it, but that was about the extent, and I only had about five feet of leeway.

Six of them escorted me to the little courtyard I'd seen earlier, letting me out for some fresh air. The fences were high and looked sturdy. There were guards on towers with guns, and others on the nearby walls. I took a few moments to look around, holding my big steel ball. Then, I saw something. On a lark, I made my way to a series of benches.

"This seat taken?" I asked, moving over toward the girl I recognized. A few others bristled, moving in my direction as I went over to her.

"Oh, sir?!" she said, snapping out of her own world and looking up at me with wide eyes.

"Siaza, you know him?" an older lady asked, hackles up as I laid the metal ball down.

It occurred to me that I'd never paid attention to her name, and that stung a bit. I'd always thought of her as the maid, and never even thought to ask her. Even while I was talking to Commander Loran, I'd only given him a description of her. That was . . . unbecoming of me, improper.

"Sir, how are you here?"

"Please, call me Percival. No need for any formality at this point," I said as I took a seat. "Saw them taking you and tried to follow to figure out where they were taking you. It was not my brightest move."

All around people looked at me and simply blinked. Then, the one who'd asked Siaza if she knew me began to laugh. She went on for a solid minute, and a few others joined her.

"You really are an idiot, aren't you?" the woman asked.

"I've been called worse," I assured her.

Siaza sat there with her hand on her face. "It's my fault you're here? That's . . . You shouldn't be here; I should be here."

"*Here* shouldn't be here either, honestly, but I doubt they care that much."

Every one of the prisoners here looked half-dead—pale, slow, tired—and even those who looked newer to my eyes looked much how I felt. So, basically everyone was pale, with deep bags under their eyes, and doing as much as they could to do as little as they could. At least there were enough benches.

"I fear we may die here," Siaza said after a time.

"Don't fear," I said. "Everyone dies; and I personally have no intention of doing so easily. At any rate, giving up will weaken you. You must fight. Fight as you never have before. Fight for your own life and freedom, and have hope. Even when things seem dark, the dawn always comes."

Those benches, thankfully, had rather loose-fitting bolts holding them together. While I sat and let my fellows berate me for my stupidity, I managed to loosen one and slip it into my sleeve. A real magician could have done it better, but I was no such thing, and nobody seemed to notice. Or, at least, no one said anything.

We were soon called to go back inside, and it was time to begin my escape attempt. I was armed with a single bolt, a long list of prison-escape movies, TV shows, and documentaries, a good knowledge of how things worked, and a deep determination for freedom.

CHAPTER 30

✶

VISITOR

It took me a few days to gather together a set of basic tools, and my, were they basic. It was bits and bobs of metal or wood, whatever I could palm, whatever I could sneak into my cell. Things that were left loose near me. The bolt was the first, but it was joined shortly by a small rubber strap, a wooden stick, a scalpel from one of the doctors who'd come to take a tissue sample from my arm—yes, he cut a chunk out and healed it afterward—and a coin someone had dropped in the small outdoor area.

I also learned more about my prison. They didn't keep me floating all the time, just a lot of it. Periodically, I was let down to use the bathroom, eat, wash, etc. My enemies were also insanely lax, so poorly regulating things that even if I'd never seen the inside of a cell on Earth, I knew that I would be much more serious about regulations. They were all dependent upon magic, but magic had weaknesses for those willing to simply step around it. They were expecting spellcasting attacks or extreme physical might to aid me.

"You look terrible," Siaza said as I joined her little group outside.

Walking with the big, heavy ball attached to me wasn't really viable. It was possible, but tiring. Nor was I feeling up to it.

"You're one to talk," I retorted.

Sadly, it was true. We all looked like dog crap refried and twice baked.

"I'm alive, and so are you, at least," she said after a bit of thinking. "Heard something is happening soon."

"What?" I asked.

"Don't know, but it's going to be big. The guards and staff are up in arms about it, cleaning everything, polishing everything, working double and triple shifts."

Some of this information didn't make it to me, since I was more isolated than they were, and I also didn't really have a point of comparison. It wasn't like she'd really been here much longer, but she had others to talk to who had been here longer.

"Good? Bad?"

"Not sure," she said, shrugging.

"Details?" I prodded, hoping that she'd gotten something from the others, some tidbit about what was happening, why it was happening, or anything else. Even things that seemed unimportant could be. Changes to schedule that would matter more than I'd like to admit, or some hint a clever person might put together.

"Just that a lot of the guards look stressed, and they're cleaning the place up."

"Hmm," I said, not giving voice to my thoughts.

Sounded to me like someone was coming. Who knew what this might mean. An inspection, a visitor, or perhaps some new member of the staff in a high position, but surely one thing—a boss. People always got worked up when their boss was going to show up at work, always made sure the messes were cleaned up, that the i's were dotted and the t's crossed for the man up the pole.

It meant a lot of things, depending on who it was. They could really mess up my plans, such as they were, if they found out about them. They could improve this place, something I really didn't want. Perhaps, though, whatever it was would weaken security. Guards who were tired were less effective; guards who were stressed had other concerns.

Either way, though, I'd have to wait and see. I didn't know what the changes would be, or if they would be temporary or permanent, or even what might be changing, and all of that mattered. It grated, but without information, acting was risky. Heck, I didn't even know when the event was going to come to pass.

"Suppose we'll have to wait and see," I replied.

For the remainder of our outdoor time, I heard some of the other prisoners talking about the things they'd seen. Priya, Hain, Lotar, and John, and their names were pronounced the same way they were in English. I smiled. I made sure to learn their names as best I could, and their stories. I needed to know who these people were and where they were from. If I could escape, I could help them all.

When the time came, I picked up my big iron ball and walked back to my room, feet calloused and back straight. My hands were also shaky; it was something I couldn't control. Once the door to my cell was closed again, the ball off, and the floating field put into place, I all but passed out.

I'd been raised among nobility, taught the arts of war at a school known for making soldiers and knights, and I knew the need of the strong to keep looking strong. If I faltered, if I looked broken and weak, the others would lose heart, hope. And they needed hope like water or food in this place. Without hope we might wither and die. If I could project just a bit of strength when they saw me, then perhaps not all hope would be lost. For it wasn't lost. If I could just get out, get to aid, this place would fall as sure as the sun sets.

My body wasn't cooperating, however. No matter how strong a front I tried to put on, I was weaker now than I'd been when I was but a young boy. Sure, I could probably still leap thirty feet vertically and outrun a horse, but I was so much weaker physically than I'd been in so long.

I was awoken to the observation slot slamming open with a clang, my dream ending abruptly. However, I didn't open my eyes; I just listened.

"Say he found the place. Who was he with?" a voice asked. It sounded harsh, proper. Getting a feel for upper class in another language was difficult, but I'd guess whoever this was, they were both rich and powerful.

"We're not sure. We've managed to track some of his communications, and he had some with an officer who believed he was a spy, but one who wasn't actually a threat. They were watching him before he came here, chasing after some thin girl who'd been working where he was staying. The theory was he was with one of the human kingdoms, concerned about some of our rhetoric, but not here to actually cause trouble. He didn't even try to access any facilities other than this one, just looked at some schools. They thought he was harmless."

"No spy is harmless. We'll need answers. The girl?" That sounded like a political statement, something a senator or representative would say.

"Nothing notable. As far as we can tell, she's not connected with anyone other than him. Technically, she's even within the legal limit to be allowed to be in society, though only barely. Something irritated someone, and they had her brought in. The doctors are none too pleased about that, but they're accepting of it for now."

"Is she undergoing treatments?"

"No, her blood is thicker than we've had success with so far."

"Change that."

"Yes, High Leader, as you command."

I really should have learned more about the titles in this place. Leader was a political one. I knew that. I knew several people holding variants of the title. The base was something like a mayor, or the like, then another that was like governor or regional head, a third was used for their own council members sometimes, but honestly, they all got jumbled in my head, and I wasn't exactly at my best.

They left, and I continued listening. There were one or two other cells on this block that were also under lockdown like I was—two on the same side of the hall as me, and three on the opposite, if I wasn't mistaken. I didn't know who was in them, but there were multiple outdoor schedules, and I'd heard them moving those two as well. Sadly, the walls were thick enough that the conversations were muddled, and I only managed to understand some basic questions from the people there, some of the place names and technical terms unfamiliar enough to be lost in the muffling of thick walls and doors.

CHAPTER 31

✶

OUT OF THE CELL

It was a few hours after the visitor left that I heard it, or rather didn't hear it. The hall was so quiet, so silent. There was only one person pacing, only one person breathing out in the hall. The afternoon was waning, as far as I could tell, and whoever it was, was moving slower than usual, plodding if anything. Then the plodding stopped.

For the first time, I heard what I'd been waiting for—the sound of a breath slowing, slowing, then, a snore. It seemed our guards were exhausted from their long trial, and we were deemed compliant. After all, though the people locked up in this hall were more dangerous, there'd not been a single incident since I showed up, not so much as a raised voice. Heck, I'd barely heard any words from the other cells.

The time had come for me to get out of here, and that meant the annoying anti-gravity trap I was in. I'd done just a little exploration, and it had a small flaw. I was already familiar with this method of disabling those of us with superhuman physical capabilities.

Newton wasn't known in this world, but his laws still applied, every action had an opposite yet equal reaction. I focused on resisting the magic—something I'd not bothered with before—and this did in fact weaken the trap significantly. But, to fully escape, I needed something altogether more important—shoes. Lucky for me my captors had provided me with a pair.

Both the shoes and my clothes were wrapped in a bundle. I needed as much weight in this thing as I could get. There would be only one attempt, and I couldn't afford for it not to work. Exhausted as I was, I gave it my all, spinning the bundle above my head faster and faster before finally hurling it against the wall. It hit with a thud, but there was no reaction from the guard sleeping somewhere in the nearby hallway.

Forces interacted, the action had a reaction, and I began to move. Not much, but a small jolt, pushing me away from the wall and toward the small sink in my cell. I focused on the magic resistance, trying to keep the trap from reasserting itself, and not just because I didn't want the guards to find me in the morning and wonder why I was in nothing but my underwear.

"C'mon, c'mon," I whispered, hand reaching.

I felt cold steel as my fingers just barely brushed the top of the sink, digging in as best I could as fast as I could, a grip for life and freedom, less than an inch on a slippery sink edge the only thing standing between me and whatever these people had planned. It was enough.

"Gotcha," I said as I pulled myself to it, wrapping my hand around the fixture as best I could and trying not to shout in joy at the small victory. Behind me the bundle I'd thrown was already being pulled back toward the center of the room, it seemed there was some small force in that direction, though I'd not felt it myself. I should have guessed.

A quick movement under an edge, pulling and reaching, and I had my tools. They were nothing more than roughly shaped bits of scrap metal, but they were the right size and shape and had sharp enough edges that they might just be enough.

The next iffy part came then. The tools went into my mouth, held between my teeth, and I positioned myself, hanging off the side of the sink like a monkey. This was the bigger risk. I might miss where I was aiming, or I might not be able to hold on when I got there. Biting down on the small metal bits I held in my teeth, I leapt.

Range this time wasn't an issue, as even weakened I could leap this room without trouble, and I did. As I hit the door, harder than I'd have liked, I found the problem. I had only fractions of a second to grab a hinge and hold on for dear life. My nails held tight, and the tips of my fingers kept my body in place even as the rest of it began to float away.

The lock was a bust; that much I knew. But the hinges looked mundane, as far as I could tell, and I sincerely hoped I wasn't wrong. My first tool came to the fore—a misshapen, rough screwdriver. It didn't have a proper handle, the edges worked by hand, but it was a screwdriver. With immense care and sweat pouring off me, I pried the caps off the two metal bits that held the door in place. Had they gone with a sliding door, or some other design, I might have been out of luck, but this was standard.

As the covers drifted off, I worked in the next bit of kit. It was a simple, thin bar with a bent end, almost like a hex wrench. I was worried. If there was an alarm, this would probably set it off. I worked the piece in, and with a hard push freed the first pin. No alarm, no noise, no lights, no sound of running feet. The second pin followed moments after.

Finally, a pair of small hooks came into play, enough to work into the now open pin holes and pry the door toward me just enough that I could get it to slide out. I didn't get it the whole way, just a few inches to make sure it would hold in place, the bolt still in securely enough that the door was sort of jammed.

Switching to the handle side—though there wasn't a handle in my cell—I grabbed the edges and pushed with all my might. There was a slight scraping, a rasp as the metal moved, and the door popped from the frame and drifted into the room. Odd. I'd expected removing it to disable the gravity trap, but alas, it had not.

Another pull and I was into the hallway, naked save for a pair of briefs, without weapons other than my makeshift tools. Hesitation would get me killed, and so I ran with all I had toward the snoozing guard. He'd leaned up against a wall, the sound of my bare feet padding on the floor not disturbing him one bit.

It had been obvious this part would come, though I drew no joy from it. This guard couldn't be allowed to wake. If I were in charge of this prison, I'd have made sure the guards watching the magical people were at least a bit magical themselves, so he almost certainly had to be since he was assigned here. Nor could I risk him having any chance to raise an alarm, bringing more men than I could possibly fight in my condition and with my lack of weaponry.

He didn't even stir as I slammed the makeshift screwdriver through his eye hard enough to rock back his head. Death was instant, painless, and silent.

"Sorry," I whispered as I helped him slide to the floor, before unhooking his keys from his belt.

Immediately, I went to the nearest door. It led to a room I thought was occupied, and it didn't take long until there was a click from the key I'd used, and the door opened inward.

An old man lay there, sleeping, and as I looked on, I realized I couldn't hear him at all. Not a breath, not even a heartbeat, but his chest still rose and fell. His ears barely had points, his breathing shallow, and his skin was covered in small dark lines, reminding me of what I'd seen of death magic from priests.

When I entered, the silence hit me like a wall. This man was surely a bard, for that was the only real reason to keep him like this. At least his room didn't have a gravity field like mine did, just a bed and sink in the corner. I made it to him in two strides and gently shook him from his slumber.

His eyes snapped open, and he went through a series of apparent emotions—fear, terror, confusion, then bemusement overtook his face. I scooped him up and carried him to the door, for I had no desire to stay in this room a millisecond longer than I had to.

He laughed, coughing once. "Never thought I'd be rescued by a boy with his sack flopping in the wind."

"I have on underwear, and keep quiet," I chided, and while he obliged I could see the shaking of suppressed laughter, at least until he saw the dead guard.

CHAPTER 32

✶

A COLD WIND

"Don't suppose you know who's in these cells?" I asked the old man as I moved him to my back, doubting he could walk.

"Afraid not," he replied. "You'll have to check if you want to know. You look terrible, by the way."

"Isn't that the pot calling the kettle black?" I asked. It was one of the sayings I assumed had been transferred by one of the other reincarnators.

He laughed and then coughed. "Indeed. Their *treatments* are not really enjoyable."

"We've got a few minutes," I told him. "If you're quiet enough, you can heal yourself." I retrieved the keys and began hauling the dead guard to the old man's cell, tossing the body into the silent room. There was surprisingly little blood.

"Think I didn't try? Whatever they did is . . . not so easily fixed."

"I know some people. We'll get you some help; just hold on." I wasn't sure if that would pan out, and I could see in his eyes he heard the half-truth of it, but if it was a lie, it was one we'd need. "What's your name?"

"Morien," he said, as I slipped a key into one of the keyholes. Sadly it was the wrong one. "Let's see what we can do about you while I'm here, though, eh?"

As I tried key after key he began to hum, low and quietly. It was subtle, but I felt slightly better, a little stronger, like he was refilling my tank somehow. It occurred to me that he'd probably been here for a while, and he seemed smart enough, since he'd tried to fix himself up. He'd probably learned long ago how to repair normal damage. I would have in his situation, and while it wasn't much, I was still thankful.

The fifth key I tried gave a click, and the door opened. Another person, a woman this time, lay in the cell. She was unconscious, her face had the same black veins, and I bit my lip in worry.

"Hey," I called, entering and trying to shake her, but finding no response. "Shit."

"Can you take her?" asked Morien.

"Only if I put you down. Can you fix her?"

"No." He didn't say anything else, but his arms tightened a bit around me, an answer to both of my comments.

"We'll come back," I said, turning. "Do you know which prisoners might be in good enough condition to move?"

"Sorry, no," he said.

As I moved to the next door and began again, hoping to find the right key faster, I heard his voice, small and afraid. "Don't leave me here, lad. I don't want to die alone."

There was terror in that voice, like he knew that he didn't have much longer until he was like the woman, unable to wake, unable to do anything else, and we both suspected we knew what would come after that.

"I've got you, old timer. We'll see the sun again soon."

Before I could say much else there was a noise. My attention on him and to the locks had been too high, and an elven man turned the corner, eyes going wide as he saw the two of us in the hall trying to open the door. There could be no hesitation, so I charged him as fast as I could.

"HELP!" he shouted before I could get to him. It was only a second of screaming, before my fist hit his temple like a sledgehammer, but it was enough. The man went down like a sack of potatoes, but it was too late.

For a brief moment there was no movement, no sound, as if the world had frozen, hanging in time like a picture in a frame, surreal, still, and quiet. Then there was an explosion of noise, scraping chairs and yells.

"Hold on!" I called out to Morien as loud as I dared; though there was no need. The old man was already gripping me as tight as he could, voice continuing the tune that seemed to help.

We screamed through the halls like an arrow loosed, sweat pouring off me as I pushed my exhausted body as hard as I could, legs screaming, heart pounding like a drum. Twice people moved into the hall near us, looking for what was happening. Twice they met my clotheslined arm as I passed, not slowing to see if it had dropped them properly or not.

I only knew one exit to this place, only one I'd been to, so I headed for it.

"Need a shield if you can," I called a few seconds before we reached it. "This is gonna be rough."

The song in my ear shifted, and a haze formed around me. There was no time for further discussion as the door appeared at the end of the hall. Though, the lyrics sounded suspiciously like he was saying "the crazy bastard."

We hit it like a cannonball of magic and flesh. This door was meant to hold in weakened normal people, not a physical magic user who was running at full speed covered in a shield. While we had slowed almost to a stop, the door still broke from the frame, the wood splintering and steel brackets bending, neither forged nor enchanted for this purpose.

See the sun we did, for it was day, and the yard was full of people. Dozens of prisoners looked at us as we exploded into the exercise area, scared eyes darting our way, voices stopped, and everyone looked up as my feet hit the ground and the sun's rays kissed our faces like a welcoming parent.

A beat later the ground under me exploded, tossing me like a ragdoll and throwing Morien from my back. It seemed at least one of the guards here had magic and the mind to use it quickly. As I tried to rise, tried to do anything, I felt myself hoisted. While I did my best to resist, the spell came on quick, pulling me into the air.

"Seize them! Multiple injured or dead. This escape attempt is—"

A scream hit the man holding me, and I saw Morien standing. He looked ragged, exhausted, hair falling across his lined face as toothpick legs pulled him up.

"Run, you fool boy! The rest of you lot, sing with me!" Already guards were pouring out the door I'd burst from, and others were converging on us.

"Morien!" I screamed at him as I pulled myself up, but he waved his arm at me harshly, toward the nearby fence and the forest beyond.

He launched into song, and I recognized it from one of my lessons. It was a children's tune about a small group of birds striking down a fearsome beast. Other voices joined in as I followed his direction and ran, even uttering the few bars I could remember as I went.

"Even the beast knew not how this could be so, let the cold winds blow, let the cold winds blow," I called as I leapt as hard as I could, barely clearing the fencing.

Behind me I heard someone else, the doctor who'd been there when I'd awoken. "You'll never handle that many. Stop!"

I didn't see it, for I'd made it well into the trees before it happened, but there was a sound like an explosion, followed by what could only be described as a squelch and a freezing wind through the woods.

Once more I ran with all my might, pushing further than my body seemed to think possible, and the distance I'd cleared was impressive. Then I heard fast footsteps approaching behind me. My dodge to the left came not a moment too soon as a bullet flew past my head.

"Dozens dead, *dead*!" I heard someone boom behind me, getting closer.

Another dodge behind a tree, and I saw my pursuer, a guard by the looks of it, with two more close behind.

"They were friends, comrades, all because you wanted to escape—even the old man and several of the prisoners—and for what?" His fist hit the tree, ripping a chunk away.

"Freedom," I replied, moving quick between the trees and trying failingly to gain distance, "and to stop your madness."

"Well, it's over. I hope you enjoyed it, for these will be your last moments." As he spoke, two additional men sped into the clearing, their uniforms different from that of the three guards. As they swiftly approached, his fist caught me, slamming me up into the air and leaving me sprawled on the ground.

"Found him," one said into his wrist.

"Indeed, we . . . Who are you?"

"Step away from him," the other newcomer said. These two wore dark uniforms, not black but a deep green with brown notes in them.

"This is the prisoner who's murdered several of our men. He is not leaving these woods," said the guard. "Identify yourselves."

"Step away," the newcomer repeated, not answering "He's coming with us."

"He's not getting away with it!" the guard shouted before lunging, clearly unable to accept the idea that I'd be taken from him.

I couldn't have dodged, but I also didn't need to. As the guard grew closer, a dome sprung up around me.

"That one's mine," came the familiar voice of the ambassador, and the cold wind from before seemed like nothing compared to the ice in his voice.

There was only a beat as the guard who'd gone for me and his two followers looked at the man as he moved into sight. Their eyes bulged in fear upon seeing his face, but neither spoke before the ambassador waved his hand, and the three enemy soldiers popped like balloons.

"And I don't like what's mine being messed with." He walked over to me, looking down, voice going back to the jovial laugh. "Anyone had the chance to tell you, you look like shit, kid?"

"Someone might have mentioned it, once or twice."

CHAPTER 33

✶

REPORTING CRIMES

It was only a few moments before a healer was standing over me, his hands working.

"They've been draining him of blood. Crude, but effective," the caster said.

"Evidently not," the ambassador retorted.

"We have to go back and quickly," I interjected. "The thing they're doing. We have to free those people. It's some kind of experiment. They're doing testing, and then . . . I'm not sure exactly what they're trying to do, but it's bad. There's a girl . . ."

"Of course there's a girl . . . Look, kid, this isn't what we're here for at the moment. We're here to rescue you, not assault some weird prison."

"Whatever they're doing, it's fatal. Black veins creeping across the skin, and that girl, she helped me. Without her aid, I might not have found the answers you were looking for. This isn't some flight of fancy, or crush. We owe her a debt, and it would be a poor showing to let them kill her."

Something I said made the ambassador freeze. "Black veins? Specifics now, please."

"I don't have them," I said. "It's not something I'm familiar with, but some kind of testing. They're gathering up the weaker blooded members of their country and putting them through those tests."

"Did they seem to increase the power of magic?" he asked, voice deadly serious.

"Not that I could tell, but again, I didn't really see. There was a bard there. He was dying, said he couldn't fix it. Pretty sure he blew himself up helping me escape. His name was Morien."

For a long moment the old elf looked at me, eyes for once not showing a hint of amusement. Then he pulled out a small contraption that looked suspiciously like a walkie talkie.

"Boss."

"Yes?" said a voice a few moments later.

"Potential magic imbuement on the more human of their people. Results are, well, what they always are."

"Are you sure, Chien? We've not seen anyone try that in quite some time, not in numbers, at least. Everyone knows the results." I noticed the wince at being called by name. He'd successfully avoided telling me his name before now.

"Black veins under the skin, a bard blowing up. Not a hundred percent, but possible."

"Very concerning. Have you retrieved Percival? Have they done anything to him?"

"Nothing that can't be fixed, but this is insane," I interjected when I saw Chien press the button again. The elder, Chien, gave me a look that warned me not to do that again.

"I should hear it from the horse's mouth, then, if you don't mind. What can you tell me?"

My slightly displeased caretaker handed over the piece of equipment, along with another warning look.

"It's human, or elf experimentation, and fatal, and they know it. I get the feeling they're also doing it to clear out the undesirable elements of their country, very we-make-the-trains-run-on-time, in a way." That comment got me a weird look and a lot of silence from my rescuers, along with a longer pause before their boss came back on.

"Any idea who is responsible?"

"They had a visit from someone they called a high leader, but I didn't get a name."

"There's only one, Percival." With that, he was done speaking with me. "Chien, do you have the forces to take the prison?" He took the communicator back.

"I mean, I'm here, so yes," he said, eyebrows crooked at the inquiry.

"Do so, and gather the evidence. As for the perpetrators, I leave them to your discretion, but if what I'm hearing is true, there's little need for them. It's been made clear again and again what the punishment of forcing mana imbuement is, and if they've not learned from several millennia of examples, well, that's their problem."

"Mind sharing the details on what you found in the capital, kid?" the ambassador asked.

I related the story—the colleges, the one that was altering elves to look like humans and teaching them our language—basically all I'd found there and how I'd found it all. I even told them about Commander Loran and how he didn't seem the worst of them all. Didn't know if that would change things, but I did anyway.

"Right, thanks. Now, I'm going to go and rip that prison apart real quick. You wait here."

"That's not happening," I replied to his order.

"Excuse me?"

"I'm going back in there with you. Maybe I'm not much of a threat in comparison, but I'm still responsible."

He looked at the healer, who responded with a shrug. "Mostly he's just missing blood. We can shove a nutrient drink down his throat and fix the worst of that pretty quickly." That didn't seem to make Chien any happier.

"Fine, kid, but try not to get in the way."

"Don't suppose you guys have a few weapons hanging around that I could borrow?" I inquired.

They didn't. This team had mostly been put together for tracking, and while they had a few blades and a couple of single-shot pistols, none were really of the kind I liked to use. My benefactor, though, did something I didn't expect. It took him a few moments, but he literally pulled iron from the dirt, along with a few other materials I recognized as synthetics, and wove me a proper sword. It wasn't enchanted, but it seemed perfectly balanced and fit my hand like it was made to.

"I really need to learn that trick," I said as I finished the nutrient drink I'd been given with a wince.

"Wrong kind of magic, and nowhere near enough time to teach you. Now, let's not let our friends languish any longer, shall we?"

CHAPTER 34

★

THE RESCUE: PART ONE

We moved, and we were lightning fast. I had fled, naked and hopeful, through these woods what felt like moments ago. Now I was returning with a jacket one of the men had loaned me, no pants, and a shining new blade in hand. This time I was not acting as a spy, and I was unafraid, for I was the flank of a conquering force.

Of course, at least at the beginning, I had to do little, for beside me the ancient wizard was uninterested in taking prisoners. Before we'd properly left the shade of the trees, lances launched from his hands, and the guard posts exploded. The fence I'd jumped in flight were ripped to ribbons before I'd taken a step. And the guards themselves? Well, they fared poorly. Some survived, but all were down within a second.

My companion was having no resistance as we approached. His voice boomed.

"Surrender, lay down, do not resist, and you will be evaluated. Fight, and you shall die." This was not a request, not some diplomatic plea. It was the word of both a judge and executioner.

The door I'd come out of was still open, and outside the building was being . . . well, taken apart brick by brick. I wasn't sure how he was planning to keep anyone from running, or if he was, but that wasn't my concern. A quick look around confirmed that my personal target wasn't outside, so I moved inside.

I hadn't been held prisoner here for very long, but it was long enough to get a general idea of the layout, and long enough to know where the non-magical people were being kept. I made a beeline for those cell blocks, a few of the men in our party followed me, all of us with weapons in hand.

The halls weren't empty. Most of the prisoners had smartly fallen to the floor and were covering their heads, but some were still a bit stunned, as were several of the guards. Unfortunately for those guards, none of us were feeling particularly merciful.

"Down now!" I shouted as we burst into a hall. A line of people in the drab clothes they'd been issued on one side were being yelled at by men in uniforms. The prisoners, used to being given orders, fell as one. The guards, however, were used to issuing orders.

I would not delude myself. Several had stout clubs in hand, looking up in surprise as we entered, and for the second time they didn't follow instruction. Most just looked up in surprise as I shot down the hall, bare feet barely touching the floor.

The first died with a spray of blood, my brand-new sword slicing through him like a hot knife through butter. Before he hit the floor, I was upon the second of four, whose hand and weapon were coming up. He was no mage or a physical magic user, as far as I could tell. He stood no chance unless I gave him one. I did not. The third guard looked like he was going to shout, but a quick thrust to his chest and a violent twist of my blade stopped his breath.

The final guard in the troop had seen the first fall and had decided that perhaps he didn't want what we were bringing, falling to the ground, hands covering his head.

"Keys," I said. A single word understood; the man quickly produced a keyring.

It took me only a few seconds to release one of the prisoners and put his cuffs onto the guard. The man I'd released was one I'd been introduced to out in the yard. John.

"It's over. Free the others, and keep that guard alive. It's not me you'll have to answer to if you don't." The building shook with perfect timing. "It's him now. Where is Siaza?"

"Don't know," John said. "They took her to the medical wing a few minutes ago . . . Is it really?" I only heard the latter part as I turned to run in the general direction he'd indicated.

"Yes," I shouted back, as I pushed through an open door.

There were windows lining the way to the medical ward—*were* being the operative word. I knew the general direction I was heading, if not the specific location. Outside, things were happening.

I couldn't see all of it from where I was, but it looked like pieces of the building, including the windows, were being ripped apart layer by layer. Some kind of blue haze was held over us in the distance, and outside, there were a lot of flying projectiles. Several of the guards had gotten guns, which sounded quite ineffective and didn't look to be doing anything but getting attention directed at them, attention they were sure to regret, if briefly. Two or three of them were also casting, hands tossing out energy to some point above that I couldn't see. However, I did see when the bars from one of the nearby windows ripped themselves from the building and flew at him, leaving something behind that looked rather like spilled Ragu.

Personally, I didn't really have the choice to be merciful, not wanting to let a threat actually stop me again. On the other hand, the leader of this little disciplinary expedition didn't seem to care much. That was a bit concerning, but also understandable. He'd been around for long enough to know that there were people who might get a lucky shot, and if they were trying, I don't know if I would give them even a breath of a chance to continue. It seemed brutal, but I wasn't sure it was wrong.

Also, these were psychopathic, experiment-happy madmen, who'd even been given a chance to surrender, so . . . fuck 'em.

Ignoring the bits of building bubbling away into the air, I moved. At this point, most of the people had fallen into one of two groups—those who were laying on the ground, hiding, and those who were acting out and running around shouting. The latter, at least, seemed interested in getting to the fight, which looked like it was outside, so we met little resistance as we moved.

The medical wing didn't look nearly as much like a prison as the other areas of the building. It was slightly brighter and less, well, not clinical, but less *institutional.* Finding Siaza wasn't difficult. I heard her well in advance. From one of the rooms down the hall, there was screaming and calls for aid in a voice I recognized clearly.

I didn't bother opening the door. Instead, I kicked it so hard that it simply left the hinges. It hadn't stood a chance. Inside, I saw the doctor I'd met when I first came in, standing over a set of syringes, with one in his hand. Siaza was bound to a nearby table by another figure I vaguely recognized, the guard who'd brought me in.

"It's over! Step away," I told them, not concealing the anger in my voice. The others who'd been following me were still a hallway or two back.

CHAPTER 35

✶

THE RESCUE: PART TWO

I immediately recognized the two as Dr. Palan and one of the enforcers, Ilan, the latter I'd met only when he'd knocked me out and brought me in. From the looks of things, I'd gotten here just in time too.

"Step away, surrender, and live."

"Or what, you'll stop us?" asked Ilan. I knew he was strong and fast, potentially stronger than me.

"I will, or the others will, and you won't get a better deal than this one."

"Oh, I think we will," said Dr. Palan. "My newest serum should work wonders! Still a few kinks in it, perhaps, but worth letting us go, I assure you. I just need proof . . ."

There was enough room that we all understood if anyone moved too much, it would result in a fight, but the doctor still tried to cast something on me. It slid off me like water on a duck's back.

"Nice try, but no."

"Magic resistance? But it worked fine on you before."

"He allowed it, doctor," Ilan explained, reaching for a short baton at his hip and letting go of Siaza. "A spy indeed."

We both moved at the same time, speeding at one another and exchanging several blows. The sword I'd been given held up without any issue, which was certainly surprising, indicating it might not just be normal steel, but his baton held up well too. He was fast, at least as fast as I was, and strong too. Perhaps a bit stronger than me, but my weapon was longer, and I'd fought those more potent than myself before. As we split, I noticed that he had several shallow cuts on his arms, and I had a bruise forming where he'd managed to just barely touch the outer part of my leg.

"Not as easy as sneaking up behind someone, huh?" I teased.

There were ways to make people mess up, depending on how good they were. Anger was one of them. Fury seldom helped in a fight, particularly one like this, where keeping your cool was of paramount importance. So I kept my cool. I had done it before and could now. These two were dangerous, and I'd seen monsters before. The only difference was that these monsters looked like people.

Another bolt zipped past my head as we closed again, and the priest moved toward the girl. I knew it was a ploy. That was obvious, but I still couldn't allow it to happen. So I moved to the side, trying to get closer, circling my enemy.

Ilan was left-handed, meaning his best attacks were coming from his left, my right. So we circled. He wouldn't let me get too close without pulling in, but I was close enough that the doctor would be threatened if he moved to her.

"I could just kill her, you know," Dr. Palan said.

"Perhaps, but would that be right? You said you were here to help people, but all I've seen is torture, pain, and death. Your experiments are doomed to fail, and you know it. Even the *improvements* are still fatal, aren't they? Or damaging to the extreme. It's desperation—desperation and evil creeping in."

"Don't listen," Ilan hissed. "He's trying to get in your head."

"Evil?! By trying to save our race?"

"Evil, killing an innocent girl who shouldn't even be here." I saw him wince, and I knew I had him.

"Shut up," Ilan said through gritted teeth, swinging at me.

Anger, and doubt for the priest, words giving advantages that blades would struggle with. The fighter surged, but sloppier, misjudging the range by mere fractions of an inch. It was enough. The tip of my blade danced up and down, circling around his strike and into his arm. Muscles slipped beneath the tip and were sliced like meat at a butcher and severed clean.

"Ilan!" Doctor Palan shouted, turning to heal his injured companion.

The hissing warrior tried to step back, his left arm limp as the doctor moved in. It wasn't like I wasn't here anyway. If they were going to keep fighting, so would I, and a simple thrust was all it took. Fights were like that—blows that could kill in an instant meant that passes were short, the results final and swift. It wasn't some exciting clash like on old TV shows, unless the opponents were very similar or one was humoring the other. No, it was quick, dirty, and brutal.

"Ah!" was the last thing Ilan said as my blade entered the bottom of his throat and went up and through, dropping him like a sack of potatoes.

"You murdered him! It was all a trick! No, I won't let you destroy our work!" The doctor sent a bolt flying that even through my resistance made my arm go numb, and he lunged.

But he was no faster or stronger than any other man. Sure, I was without my right hand, my sword falling to the floor, but I could still function well enough. As he moved, my left grabbed the hand he'd brought up over Siaza, who was screaming, still tied to the table. It was the hand with the syringe, and I turned it, plunging the needle into his own belly before I slammed the plunger down. A black liquid shot from the syringe into his gut faster than he could react.

"What have you done?" he asked in shock.

"What you'd have done to her," I responded before punching him. Really there was no reason to leave him alive other than the fact that our leader would decidedly want to speak with him.

"Sir?" she asked, voice shaking.

"It's okay," I assured her. "Everything's going to be fine." Though, I had not a single idea if that were true. "Did they give you any of those shots?"

"No . . ."

"Good."

The doctor was out cold, so I took my time releasing her from the straps. I could have cut them like an action hero, but why subject her to that stress when I could act calm and unconcerned.

Things were quiet for a while after that. The battle outside had ended, and I had a feeling I knew which way the tide had turned. My instincts were confirmed a few moments later when the ceiling literally came apart piece by piece, pulled away above us.

"He's one of the ones in charge here," I shouted to the airborne elf, pointing. "And those are what they were giving them. Pretty sure he's a priest, and I opted to give him some of his own medicine."

"Poetic," Chien replied. His voice sounded like it was coming from only a few feet above us rather than a shout. "I'll speak to him in a bit. You two get outside and join the others."

Bits of metal reformed in the air as the old wizard brought them into new shapes, binding the doctor tightly in a sarcophagus that left only his face open and no locks that I could see. For some reason, I doubted he'd be let out anytime soon.

That wasn't my problem though. Instead, I scooped up the girl I'd come to save and jumped out of the crumbling building.

CHAPTER 36

✶

DEBRIEF

It wasn't long before the debriefing began. The guards were in their cages, the prisoners gently corralled into a side area where one of the buildings was still slightly standing. I found the elder, Chien, sitting by the captives flipping through pages, a frown creasing his brow.

"This is appalling," he said, reading the notes. "Not what I feared, but appalling. I'm no master of this form of magic, but even to me it seems obvious this was doomed to fail. You said that priest was responsible?"

"Indeed," I indicated as he spoke, picking up another pile of notes. "Some of the people we rescued—"

"I noticed," he said, cutting me off.

"Yes. Is there anything you can do for them?" I asked.

"No, that isn't my magic; though I'll see that they get the best help I can offer. I see the girl you wanted to save is well though." He gave me a rakish smile.

"I'm not interested in her that way," I replied, frowning.

"You sure? I think she'd be into it."

"I'm betrothed already."

"A betrothal isn't a marriage; it can be broken off," he said, seeming to regard it as a game.

"It could, but going after another girl would seem more akin to betrayal by my reckoning. It's not even worth considering."

"Ha! Knew I liked you for a reason. I may not share your desire for marriage, but I do at least appreciate your loyalty and honesty. You're a good kid."

"Thanks, I guess . . ."

"At any rate, I will have some priests I know look at those folks. No promises on results, but we'll do what we can. Perhaps one of our prisoners may be able to aid in that regard."

With a motion, the steel coffin containing the doctor was brought over, the top opening to reveal his face. He looked rancid, like he'd been awake for a month and was right on the cusp of death.

"That's . . . It's only been an hour," I said, surprised.

"Good afternoon, doctor."

"You . . ."

"Yes, us. We beat you. My young friend here gave you that drug. Is this violent response normal?" Chien inquired.

"Should fade a bit in . . . a few days. The other injections were for the pain and to help rest, along with speeding the process. My, it hurts." He didn't even try casting at us, which I was thankful for.

"Well, your notes indicate your subjects die regularly, but there's no way to reverse it mentioned. If you know of one, we might be able to aid you, and the others, of course."

"Never found one. Our focus was on stabilizing the process, not curing the failure. I . . . might survive. There have been a few cases that did well enough . . ."

"Shame. Did you never look into it?"

"We did once or twice, trying to alleviate . . . Damn, I'm too tired. The notes you want are in the files from my office, furthest from the door, bottom shelf."

"I thank you for that. You may rest now." With another flick, Chien closed the coffin again and moved it to the side.

"Don't suppose you've heard back from . . . well, you know." I didn't want to be too clear, as that individual had made it very clear he didn't want to be identified, and some of the guards might have enhanced hearing.

"I understand he got into that school, and based on what he found, he has been hunting down several of the admins, physicians, and soldiers involved. He hasn't begun the removal of them yet."

"Really?"

"If someone like that needs to act, they prefer to be thorough. Your input may be helpful when things go down, if you're willing."

"That tracks, I suppose, but how can I be of aid when the action begins? I'm afraid it might be a bit beyond what I'm capable of."

"Not what I meant, kid. You won't need to fight; though you might see a bit of it. What we really need you for is Commander Loran. It seems he really isn't involved in this mess, as far as we can tell, and somebody is going to need to be around to step forward once the doing is done."

"You're just going to what, hand over the whole country to him on my recommendation? That seems a bit risky."

"Oh, he'll have good reason to behave, and to restructure as we tell him, assuming he can keep control, which shouldn't be too hard after what is going to happen. It'll be better than the alternative. Ever seen a nation that loses its leader too suddenly, kid? See, things go wrong, and they go wrong in a hurry. Nobody knows who's in charge, nobody knows what to do with themselves, or if they should be in charge, or if their faction should. Then they start thinking maybe that is how it should be. Civil war often follows shortly after that. It's worse when the leader is someone like Scoran. He put everything into himself, all the trust. All the people love him. That will be changing soon."

"I'm not so confident they'll abandon him so easily. Nationalism can be a poison that's hard to come back from. Even so, and even should you shove their faces in what they've been doing, they may have a hard time accepting it. It's not like they were seeing it all too closely, and it will come out that you just showed up and started killing and ripping things up. You'll look like a bully."

"Wow, you've not spent enough time among us. When ancients act, all elves know to listen."

"You've done this kind of thing before?"

"A few times over the years. I don't like it; nobody else does either. Nor do we actually want to take over all the other cities and small states around us. Atal could, but it's not worth it, and I was there when we signed the treaties that let each loose. There were requirements that this place broke, so if I were in the mood, I could just reclaim all of it and be done, but . . . I don't want to."

"Fine, I'll help where I can. When are we doing this?"

CHAPTER 37

✶

RETURN

There were things I liked and disliked about my current employer. What I liked was that he was quite decisive, knowing what he wanted to do, and when and how. What I disliked was that he was also a bit of a bastard, but he wasn't cruel. Moreover, I hated the constant jokes, like the one I was pretty sure he was playing on me now.

We were flying back to the city. This wasn't because we couldn't teleport, which I was told might be possible, but because there was no rush and we were "looking for more trains," which I suspected meant giving me a hard time.

"Really, can you do nothing about the vertigo? It feels like my inner ear is tumbling down a mountain."

"You get used to it."

"I should hope not," I replied. "I don't want to do this ever again."

"Well, you can't do better."

"I heartily disagree. I can and have done better. My planes are a hundred times better than this!" I shouted, still feeling like I was in the wash cycle.

"Suppose that's true enough, though that's not really you flying. That's just the machine flying and you being along for the ride."

"Like I am right now?" I said, trying to keep my balance and not succeeding in any meaningful way.

He laughed, and I was even more sure he was screwing with me again. After a time, though, the ride did at least settle a little, and I took in the view of the land below us. It was forested, but with a lot of flakes, like reclaimed marshland or something.

"No trains," I observed.

"No, indeed. Well, at least the view is better than it used to be. This place was never much to my liking."

"Should we worry about being seen?" I asked as we pulled over the city, slowly lowering.

"I'm quite capable of controlling the light around us. They cannot see us," he assured me as we landed. "Nor can they hear us, until I allow it."

I knew we were going to meet up with the king, but things were clearly different than the last time I'd been around here. The city wasn't in full panic, and people were still moving about, but there had been changes. The most obvious was the number of soldiers.

Everywhere I looked there were men in uniforms. Some were even donning armor and pointed helmets. That seemed odd, but I supposed the reasoning was sound. A blow from above would still be pushed away from the face. It was one of those weird things that seemed to carry over, like maid outfits or certain sensibilities. Perhaps just a repeating pattern through the multiverse, perhaps some influence from one of the several transmigrators.

"Something catch your eye?"

"The helmets."

"Hmm, think the boss mentioned them offhand a few times, but we never used them. The southerners are a bit weird, latching onto the strangest things that were just ideas and sketches."

"Why? Surely some of the information for the real things would be available. I mean they could just ask you."

That got me a hearty laugh. "It may be easy for you to talk to me, but that is not the normal situation. I'm often quite busy, and I don't like a lot of people."

Now it was my turn to look surprised. "Really?"

"Yeah, other than a few diplomatic trips now and again—and man, are those uncommon by most people's reckoning—I mostly keep quiet. Run a lot of paperwork, put out fires, work on a few personal projects, but time seems to fly faster every year."

We were approaching the base that I knew housed Commander Loran but weren't stopping for some reason. The guards and soldiers didn't even acknowledge us. Then it hit me that we were probably still invisible, which was a neat trick, if nothing else.

"Maybe you should take a vacation," I suggested sometime later, as we entered the building, moving between people.

"That's what this is. I've had basically zero paperwork during this trip, and my, do I love it. Also beats my normal break, which is showing up to flatten whatever monster has caused too much trouble. Doesn't happen often, and I try to let the military take care of it first, but if they can't . . ."

"Why not just do it yourself?" I asked as we opened the office door.

"Because it would stifle the growth of people as a whole," answered the old elven king, sitting in the chair before Commander Loran's desk and flipping through some papers. "Perhaps it seems cruel, but you have to let them stand on their own, if they're not to suffer in the long term, even if it means some die."

The owner of this office was here too. I was guessing we had been pulled into an invisibility or hearing bubble, however that worked. The commander looked at us, face pale and clearly stressed to the limit. Of course, two pure elves of indeterminate age were now in his office, one of which had been rightly pissed off lately.

"Commander," I said nodding to him.

"They told me you were spying on a number of sensitive things and were captured. I'm actually supposed to be going before a board of my superiors shortly about it," he said.

"Most of your superiors will be dead by sunrise," the unhappy elven king sitting across from the commander informed him. "Really, nearly all of them. We're here to discuss your taking over after the fact. There needs to be stability, and people need to know why it happened. You're going to inform them of all of this."

"Of course, Your Majesty. Thank you once again for showing yourself to me. I assure you, we've no desire to anger you in the least. If you merely stepped forward, you could rule yourself—"

"If I wanted to rule, I would. No, it is better if you do it, and keep others from knowing I'm still around."

"I understand, Your Majesty." I had a feeling that if he told the man to shoot his best friend, he would, but in this case that might actually be reasonable.

"Good, now, I have some people who will be available for you. Pick some of them out and get them here before everything starts happening. The soldiers seem to have noticed that I broke into one or two places."

"Well, you did level that one building," he pointed out, though kept his tone quite polite.

"Why'd you do that?" I inquired.

"To destroy some of the equipment," he said. "Now, Commander Loran, pick your new subordinates so we can get on with this."

CHAPTER 38

✶

A SPOONFUL OF MERCY

Once Commander Loran called the men he wanted to meet him, insisting as strongly as he could, the process began.

To be honest, I was surprised at how it went down. The old king had identified all the people he wanted gone, and had managed to see them summoned to one place, the ruling palace. Each received letters, either from Commander Loran or the elven king himself, through some proxy telling them to arrive at sunset.

"Why sunset?" I asked as we moved through the streets, the two ancient wizards shielding us from sight or sound. Behind us, the commander was putting together his people, keeping them out of the way and safe. Nothing would be explained until after it was over.

"Most people will be home with the increased soldiers patrolling, traffic will be low, people will be eating dinner, not going out to bother us and potentially get hurt."

"And the boss is rather dramatic when he's mad," Chien said. "The sun setting on their rule as we light the place up like a blaze. Been a while since I got to really let loose. Are we worried about anyone?"

"No. Those in the ruling palace are all high in the government. Even the assistants are part of his regime; the guards too. We're not taking prisoners, of course." The way he said it made my skin cold with the promise of terror to come.

"Hold on, we should try at least—"

The old elf turned to me, and I could see the fury in his eyes, the rage that had been buried.

"None of them would have shown mercy. Not one of them would have lifted a finger to save the girl you went out of your way to rescue, or you. Why should I?"

"And what if there's even one who is innocent? You're mad. I get that, but you can't let the anger make you do something foolish." He didn't blink; nor did I. "Don't let it get away from you. Don't cause a slaughter."

And then he paused. A man who'd seen more than I could imagine stopped, and he thought. His anger was still present. That much was clear; but he was thinking about it, so I continued.

"You said the assistants are part of it, and maybe some of them are, but some could just be caught in the middle, innocents that you'd slaughter. Even those who wouldn't do good might not have done evil yet."

"You're right," he said after a few moments. "We take out the soldiers, the leaders, then . . . well, try to capture the civil servants. If they fight, they die, but if they flee or surrender, disable. Percival, are you joining us?"

"Wouldn't miss it for the world," I answered.

"Good, you'll need these, then."

I was presented with a small box, containing two weapons of my own design, though certainly not made by me. These two were arsenals to themselves, and while the counselor had only given me a blade during our last assault, our leader here had produced pistols seemingly from nothing. They were to spec, too, larger than normal caliber, of the same design that I had made, and with a few small flourishes on the grips. Excellent work really, and to a standard I couldn't complain about. There were even a pair of holsters; though, rather than leather, they felt almost synthetic, like plastic.

"I'm going to ask for royalties if you start making these wholesale," I joked as I rotated the cylinder of one pistol. I loaded them both and holstered them.

"If I wanted to make lots of guns, I would've done so years ago," he replied with a straight face.

"Bit jealous of you two being able to do that," I grumbled.

"We couldn't at your age, if it helps," Counselor Chien said, laughing. "And if you were to make it to ours, you'd be an unstoppable force on your own, probably able to run faster than a bullet and with skin harder than steel."

"Wait, seriously?"

"We've known elves who've had abilities similar to yours. They grow slowly with time, not as obvious as outward magic, but no less dangerous. After a hundred years, most are quite powerful. A thousand? Able to do feats you wouldn't believe and resist most magic as if it were nothing to them. There are flaws to everything."

"Even yours?"

"Behind the magic and defense neither of us are more than flesh and blood. Don't you know that? We've had a long time to build our defenses, but that is how it is. Even priests who can support their own bodies to an extent, and bards who can do . . . quite frankly strange things sometimes, are limited in what their bodies themselves can do. Your reaction time is faster than mine already."

These were, of course, things I knew in an intellectual sense, but it didn't seem that way. The two elders before me seemed so far beyond me in power that it was like a child comparing themselves to a trained adult. Perhaps that was part of their power too—the perception of power. Though they also had the ability to level buildings, which really helped with the perception.

"Right, so what's the plan?" I asked.

"Stay near me, fight if you feel the need or desire," our leader informed me. "Chien, please work the edges. Everyone should be here, but look for any issues and handle as you wish."

With a nod, the counselor disappeared, and a few moments later His Majesty spoke to me.

"Thank you, by the way, for standing up to me. I was angry, too angry, and too few people will actually call me out; though, Chien might have said something if you hadn't. He knows I would've regretted it in time." Then he pulled forth a mask, slipping it over his face.

"Anger, I understand, but that was too extreme."

"Those of us who possess no human blood have perfect memories. Pain doesn't go away, not ever, and memories that hurt don't fade. I sometimes feel the deaths of my parents and other loved ones today as if it were still that day. The losses of each and every one, it . . . weighs on you. Perhaps I'm a bit immature, not having learned how to deal with it as well. I really should have, a lesson I've been taught many times, but it makes me less merciful than I should be."

"Right, well, mercy for those who need it, but we can at least agree that this regime needs to fall."

"Indeed, and there's no time like the present," he said with a smile, tossing up a small ball that flew skyward. A dome flowed down from it fast, cutting off the palace from the outside. "So let's begin."

CHAPTER 39

BARRIERS

The dome seemed to be the inciting moment for everything to go nuts. Perhaps they were expecting us. I didn't know, but as soon as the dome covered the building, men began to pour out in waves.

Spells began to fly, the two of us still unseen. I felt the wave of magic looking for people and shrugged it off. I saw the beams of light washing over the grounds, followed by what looked like planes of force erected all around the place. Single-shot rifles were brought to a few soldiers who already had shields and armor and their pointy helmets.

"Think we stirred up a hornet's nest," I mused.

"At least we found the soldiers quickly."

To my surprise, the elven king didn't just vaporize the lot of them, which I was guessing he could. Instead, the old elf strode forward, and a cloud began to billow out from one side of the field—not the side we were on, but to our right. Everyone turned and unloaded on it. Not that that did them any good. As it struck the soldiers, they fell one by one.

"Surrender," he said, voice resonating over the courtyard.

"I'm surprised you're offering," I said.

"Well, these men may or may not be guilty," the elder replied. "We can find out later."

None did surrender, though, and many began to fall. Several mages flew upward, and appeared to melt where they hovered. That put a bit of a damper on things, with some soldiers dropping their weapons and fleeing, and others looking unsure what they should do. All the while, where the cloud flowed, men and women kept falling.

As we approached the entrance, I saw bullets bouncing off the elven king's shield. He didn't even slow his pace as he moved forward. Some of these people were clearly not soldiers, but instead administrative staff, and with the cloud remaining outside, it was clear what would become of them.

Not one to be outdone, I moved away, slipping into the darkness nearby. They were all very, very concerned about the old elf taking apart their defenses, and much less worried about me. This led to an easy chance to move for targets near the backline—supporters, healers, and those who might try to run.

I could've stayed near the ground, but instead I went up, depending on the fighting to cover me. We'd entered a door that led into a massive atrium. Around us there were little balconies, overlooking, the hall below.

Pillars were carved all the way round it, like small stone trees, with vines woven around them and small, painted flowers. I leapt onto the pillars, above what would've been branches stretched out to make the arch of the ceiling, like we were in a forest. A peaceful place. Well, not anymore.

I landed on a vine, then leapt to one of the overhangs. Nearby, a man was bringing a gun to bear, so I decided to respond in kind with one of my own new weapons. I pulled, aimed, and fired in the same motion.

Normally, I would've tested weapons first, before brandishing them on a battlefield, but I really hadn't had time. As the hammer struck home, my hand was almost ripped up, the kick far harder than I'd designed in my own weapons.

BOOM!

The smell hit me a second after the shot blew a hole through my target's torso. It wasn't standard powder, but something that smelled more modern. I hadn't noticed at first, but with my experience it was clearly something slightly different. There were a lot of ways to change the accelerant, many of which were quite dangerous.

I'd have to depend on the fact that the elder knew what he was doing, and that I'd designed the thing to be overbuilt, regardless.

The next person I saw was leaving a small office, a woman, not in military uniform. She was dressed in civilian clothes and had no weapons, no spells rolling around her hands. She wasn't even heading toward the fighting, instead away from it, trying to turn into a hallway. Did she deserve to die? I didn't know, but she did need to be stopped.

So, I moved after her, a blur to any eyes that weren't enhanced, closing the distance. Two strikes. Controlled, quick, careful. One was delivered with the pommel of my sword, a disabling blow, the other a pulled-back punch to the side of her face. She was slack before she hit the ground.

Then I had to dodge, for one of their physical magic users had seen me and was coming at speed. His blade, far heavier than mine, drew a trail across the distance between us. I had to parry as best I could while I turned my blade, a full rotation of the arm which turned the parry into a thrust, one too close for him to dodge.

It was over fast, and I moved on. So, I moved along the side of the room, as fast and as quietly I could. Of course, I wasn't perfect. Once or twice a shield from my ally blocked something that was coming for me. That hurt. It was like he didn't need me here at all, like I was hardly a help at all to him. Then I cut down another attacker and got back to business.

Those I could safely disable, I did; those I couldn't, I didn't. Killing was not something I loved, not something I sought, but I'd made my peace long ago that there was a time for it, when it could be accepted. It was a tragedy, but what these people were doing was a tragedy too. It was horrible, and so was that prison. Killing was not what I sought, but they had been given a chance that the oppressed never had—to turn from their path.

As we neared the end of this battle, him below and me above, I saw an open door at the end of the atrium, and an elf appeared, flanked by guards.

"Enough," he declared, pulling forth some item, and the ground around the edges of the open area where the king was standing began to glow.

I had just a moment to see shields flicker around both of us—thick hazes of magic, probably some mix of kinetic and other forms of energy, which even seemed to lessen light—as the floor flowed, a thick barrier forming where he stood.

The two elves didn't even acknowledge me, and that was to my benefit.

"I assure you, that barrier is meant to hold even one such as you," the high leader said.

"I assure you, it is not," the ancient responded, and began casting.

Magic wavered, pushing and pulling. I could tell by the look on his face that his confidence was failing, but for the moment, at least, the barrier was holding.

CHAPTER 40

✶

FALL OF A LEADER

On one side stood a dictator, using an item to form a trap. On the other, an ancient king, power radiating from him, ripping away at the trap. The power from them both was titanic. They were examples of what masters of magic could do. Tides of power that few people saw were now working against one another, the strength of a nation against one man.

"Try as you might . . ." The elven king seemed to hesitate for a moment, seeing the small holes beginning to form.

Of course, neither of them were paying attention to me. How foolish, for I was pretty good at being the wrench in the works.

The guards were shooting guns into the trap. They seemed to do nothing at all, but as they fired, I moved. I slinked along the edge of the walkway, my enemies dead or fleeing, save for the ones who'd now shown up. The floor was littered with the dead, the broken, blood pooling and bits of plaster and stone ripped apart.

The high leader pulled out the control mechanism, adjusting it to keep the trapped ancient from advancing or escaping.

"We've been working so hard for so long, yet we have no ancient of our own to lead us. With a vial of your blood we could, perhaps, advance our cause, fix the underlying issues in the experiments we've been running," he said, almost gloating, clearly trying to get a reaction.

"Your experiments are over, your facility leveled, your men taken. Do you not realize this?" the masked ancient retorted.

There was a moment where the goading stopped. As it did I pulled up to the side of a vine-covered pillar, making sure to keep to the darkness as best I could. I'd only get one chance.

"You destroyed it? All our work?" High Leader Scoran asked.

"Personally, no, but I did order it. To be fair, I thought you were trying to induce magic. Though, had I known what you were doing, I'd have done so anyway. It is doomed to failure, and you don't even understand why."

"And I suppose you'll tell me now?" the high leader scoffed.

"No, there's no point in telling a dead man anything like that. It would take too long anyway."

"Yet I'm the one out here, and you're the one in the trap." As he spoke I could see more and more power being drawn in, though it didn't seem to be working.

"A trap with a finite amount of mana. How many units does it use per second? Fifty? A hundred? Based on the size, it can't hold more than . . . no, about a minute or two more. Then, if it doesn't stabilize to recirculate, it'll fail on its own."

"You think you know better than our artificers, the greatest in the world!"

"Hardly. There are several flaws. Never mind that though."

The banter had given me the time I needed to get in place, brace my arm, make sure I was hidden, and to aim with immense care.

BOOM!

Sure, I could have killed the high leader. I would have enjoyed it too, but no. I could have taken his guards too—a pair of shots to disable them and let me move in, but that wasn't my goal. I aimed for the item in his hands, the control mechanism.

Time seemed to move slowly around us. I couldn't see it, but a small lead projectile left the barrel in a plume of smoke and fire. Spinning like a graceful ballerina, the grooves of her skirt flared against the twist in the rifling that sent her forward. Across the hall and its stone columns she went, past the lovely decorations, over tiles arranged in frescoes, and along stairs and railings shaped of iron and gilded with silver and gold. She met her partner—that small metallic thing in the leader's hand—and brought him to join her in a shattering dance as they exploded. She also happened to tear into the hand holding it, ripping a significant chunk from the flesh and sending a middle finger flying. Nobody was perfect.

As time returned to its normal speed, I had to rush to duck behind the pillar next to me. Not a second later a pair of bullets and some sort of magical bolt slammed into it, sending shards of stone from the column flying. It was accompanied by a pained yell, so I had that going for me.

"Forgetting about someone?" I heard, even over the sound of the attacks and the scream.

The next sound I heard was difficult to describe, like a mix between a Tesla coil and the clicking on of a light. The gunshots stopped.

"What did you . . ." the high leader whispered; though, to my strong ears it was still clear as day.

"There's no need to worry. You'll be with them soon."

About that time the smell hit me, a sickening mix of ozone and burning flesh.

Thinking quickly, I popped back out to see the leader turning to run. Well, we couldn't have that, so I brought the pistol back up and put a round through his left knee. The damage was . . . more than I would have anticipated, and I was glad I hadn't aimed much higher, or he'd be very dead very quickly.

Even at that moment, the ancient elf had the trap well in hand. With nobody to manage it, increase or decrease the power as needed, change whatever setting they'd been fighting with, it was coming apart at the seams. Pieces were ripping away as lances slammed into spots in the foundation, aiming for some anchoring point that I couldn't see, but it was obvious to the man within it.

"You . . ." the injured man said from the ground. "We could have risen to our greatest heights again! We could have been immortals once more, but you do this! I was to purify our race, drive the humans back into the dirt where they belong. I was following the will of His Majesty, and now you come here to destroy and break us again, you bastard!"

"The will of the king? What do you know of the will of the king?" said king asked.

"I studied his words, his works, his desires. I knew what he wanted."

"You're an idiot," I said, pulling in front of the column and looking at the broken man.

"I was doing what His Majesty would have wanted!" he screamed back.

"You're a fool! If you read those old records, you didn't understand them," the writer in question said, removing his mask, "or you would know that what I wanted was for my people to live well and peacefully, free from monsters, not oppressed and tortured."

"That . . . It must be a lie . . ."

"No, foolish child. It's the truth, but be glad, for you do get to do my will one time, at least. Percival, would you like to?"

"No, sir," I replied. "He's all yours." I wasn't one to deny a man his revenge, and my companion had a much better claim than I did. Heck, I'd even tried not to kill the man when I had a clear shot.

"Good. Perish." Done with the conversation, the ancient lifted his hand, and wiped High Leader Scoran from the face of the . . . well, not Earth, since we weren't on Earth, so *world*.

CHAPTER 41

CLEANING UP

I would love to say that once we'd dealt with High Leader Scoran it was all over, but we had a long, long day ahead of us.

People were important. They were symbols, hubs of power and information, but they weren't everything. No, systems were built around them. Systems to control, to activate, to change this or that. The system had to come down. It had to change, and that was harder than killing one man. First, we'd start here, then the co-conspirators would do their part.

"There's a few office staff here," I told my companion as he put his mask back on. "We'll need to figure out who's who."

"Indeed, though most of them will end the same as their leader."

"I saw at least one secretary or something back there, knocked her out."

"Well, she can probably stay," he grumbled.

We could hear a few people trying to escape inside the building, but they were swiftly dealt with. Councilor Chien was there, of course, and he was no slouch.

While he was taking care of that, the ancient and I roamed deeper inside the structure. There were a few pockets of resistance, but only a few significant ones. Several officers and loyalists had holed up in the basement, where I didn't have a good way to get involved, or a good chance to do so.

I did, however, see some more action, as three men tried desperately to ambush us in a hallway. In those moments I discovered that Chien had been right—my reaction time was better. Personally, the makeshift explosives they'd thrown at us probably wouldn't have actually hurt either of us, since none of them went off, but that didn't stop me from getting shots off.

"Can you do something about those?" I asked, looking at the failed bombs. "We really shouldn't leave unexploded ordnance behind."

"Unexploded ordnance?" He laughed at me. "Sure, one second." They fell apart into some kind of powder. "I like you, kid."

"Thanks," I replied. "You seem pretty cool yourself, Your Majesty."

"Please, call me Justin," he said with a sigh. It was clear that was his Earth name.

"Not *boss*?" I joked.

"Don't take notes from Chien—well, do, but not those. He's been a joker his whole life."

"I noticed. He played a few on me, like bringing the lovely goblin girl you met along. He hid her in a box, and she popped out like a child's toy." That got me a snort of laughter.

"Still, I don't understand why they did what they did," he grumbled.

"Oh, I found that out. Apparently, you left writings about goblins—how they were rapacious monsters."

I quirked my ears. I heard something nearby.

That got me a sigh. "Fuck, left some stories behind, cribbed from old anime. Those were just supposed to be stories, not instructions. These people take everything I say too damn literally."

"Hold on," I replied, looking up. "Come out; I know you're up there."

The sound was small, but close, breathing and perhaps a pounding heart, above us.

"Please!" she called out, for it was decidedly a feminine voice. "I'm not a threat!"

I shrugged at Justin, and he replied in kind.

"Come out, then," I repeated.

The woman who climbed down from the ceiling was clearly a civilian. She had on an apron, one she'd been wearing when she fled, with pockets for combs and a couple of pairs of scissors.

"A hairdresser?" Justin asked, looking at her.

"Ah, yes, I saw to the officers and the high leader. I won't fight; not very strong."

"I did not come here to kill barbers. Go outside and lay on the grass. If you speak the truth, you won't be harmed."

"Yes, yes sir." Before she moved, though, she had a question. "Is, is it true? Is it really you?" she asked, her voice small.

"Really, who?" he replied, voice hard as stone, mask covering his features. "Surely, you've mistaken me for another, child. Now go outside and do as you were told."

"Yes, Your Maj—" At the small growl that came from him, she thought better of finishing her sentence. "Yes, sir, I will."

She headed the way we'd come, nearly running. Once I was sure she was gone, I looked at him.

"She'll tell others."

"Others have before, when they've seen me. Keeps the rumor mill going, conspiracies alive. To be honest, I like it better that way.

Gives people a story, rather than a reason to go digging in places they shouldn't. Easier to mislead them."

"My, my, leading this world's Illuminati. Didn't expect that of you," I joked.

"No, that's the Orders," he corrected.

"Sorry, wait, what?"

"Don't know why they're not allowed on Elazia, then? Oh, don't ask too many questions. Might make you a target if they know you know, or know you'd met me."

"Wait, what?!"

CHAPTER 42

✶

CONSPIRACIES AND LOST LESSONS

"You cannot leave me like this," I told Justin as we were going through the files. "The Orders!"

"Really, you should just drop it. They're not as bad as you might think, most of the time."

"Most of the time?!"

"Look, everyone has a vision, and as we get older and stronger, we start to impose that vision upon the world, whether we want to or not. The Orders do, too, and while most of their vision is fairly benign, they overstep at times. It's part of the reason human governments are the way they are, and why sometimes we have to do things like we did here today. We don't allow them in, so we get different problems than you do."

We went back and forth for a while before he got tired of arguing and did something that enforced silence over the room. My response to this was calm, mature, and reasoned. I took a piece of paper, wrote "Don't be a dick" on it, balled it up, and threw it at his head.

"I'll stop being a dick when you stop being a child," he said, breaking the silence.

"Come on! A continent-sized conspiracy. How can I not freak out?"

"Because they don't mean evil. Unlike most conspiracies, they cannot; it would weaken them immensely."

"Father was evil."

"A fair point, but neither here nor there. I don't believe there is a threat."

"I have friends and family that live there. Do you?" I said, getting serious.

"Yes."

Well, that answer threw me. Sincerely, I hadn't been thinking he would have a good response to that? Were those he cared for among the humans? The way he said it implied it was true.

"And, if I thought there was a threat," Justin continued, "I would act. Now, stop acting like a child."

"Fine, fine, but still, what is the conspiracy? I'd like to know if I should be worried, and you telling me I shouldn't be isn't enough, I'm afraid."

"The rules the Orders enforce are the thick of it. They take every priest. Did you know that? All of them join, and those who refuse seem to die a lot, don't they? They also enforce their rules on people in power."

"Like the no-forced child labor and stuff?"

"Yes, that."

"Most of that is okay, I guess, but they're, what, assassinating people who oppose them?"

"Up to a certain point, yes. They either withdraw and let them die or they kill them. Ugly, isn't it? Keeps a basic level of civilization though. Sadly, I feel they're too heavy handed." He looked around the office in the capitol building we had just assaulted. "Maybe I'm not one to talk though."

"Probably not, but I don't think what you're doing is wrong . . ."

"Always thinking you're right leads to terrible outcomes, Percival. I would encourage introspection, in myself particularly."

There was a knock at the door, and soon Commander Loran joined us. "Your Majesty, my people are ready to begin moving in and taking over. Shall I tell them who we'll be working under now?"

"You're working under yourselves."

"You won't stay?"

"No, you're quite capable of leading the people of this nation. My presence here was to solve a problem, and the problem is solved. It is better for everyone if I return to my solitude for now."

"Your Majesty, I respectfully disagree."

"Hah! Good. Disagree with me more and we'll be getting somewhere. Still, though, I told you that I wanted my involvement kept secret."

"And I've kept it," the commander said, sadly. "I was hoping you'd change your mind. Frankly, I'm not much of a politician."

"Not being a good politician is a good thing, I think, at least for the transfer. Care to help us look over some of these files?"

The records weren't as detailed as the ones from the prison, of course, at least not from what I'd heard. Justin flew through them like he wasn't even reading them, just scanning them for details, while both Commander Loran and I were being a bit more thorough.

"Reports of their . . . successes—that's what they called them. The percentage increase they're recording is minuscule, and even they admit that it caused massively shortened lifespans, like a year at most."

"Disturbingly close to mana enhancement," Justin grumbled. "Though probably for a very different reason."

"Do you know the reason, Your Majesty?" Commander Loran asked.

"Drop it. It's impossible as things are, and will only make you end up like your former boss," I told him, not wanting to hear that idea repeated.

"You misunderstand," the commander retorted. "I don't wish to repeat his mistakes, but to find some way to aid any survivors. Can it be fixed?"

"Probably not," Justin admitted. "They were ripping people apart from the inside, not properly understanding what they were doing. The 'gains' they were finding was just less genetic material to see, not more elven blood."

I watched the commander's face fall, and his eyes darkened. "Are you telling me that we were just killing them, that the government I worked so hard to maintain was simply murdering its people?"

"Yes," I answered him. "Their ideas never had a chance. There are things you can do overall, if you think increasing the amount of elven blood is important. Banning humans, trying to encourage marriages between people—it's dangerous, and prejudiced, and may lead to this outcome again though."

"No," he replied. "We'll need to change things."

"I wonder how many more times this conversation will take place," Justin mused. "We're on three or four now."

"We won't forget," Commander Loran said, looking at him fixedly.

"Perhaps, but your great-grandchildren might." It was a tired statement from a man who'd seen so many generations. It hurt me, too, for I knew I'd lost lessons that I could have learned from older men.

CHAPTER 43

✶

MEETING SIAZA

I ended up having to stick around for a few more days, not because there was anything for me to do, but because the two old-as-dirt elves were too busy to take me back home. I was hoping they had a faster way than by ship. Boats were nice and all, but I was good and ready to be back where I belonged.

For the most part, I stayed inside. A room was prepared for me at the same hotel I'd stayed, which suffered a few staff changes. There were organizational transitions all around, in fact, and no small number of arrests. Most of these were in the government sector, but not all, with some civilians pulled from their homes or places of work under charges of crimes against elvenkind, which brought a smile to my face.

There were fewer people on the street, and more at the same time. A lot had taken up staying in their homes, but I saw so many more elves that clearly had a lot of human blood running about over the course of those three days that I wondered where they'd all been before. Not all of them were from the prison, though a couple were. My former maid, Siaza, even came to visit, though not at the hotel. She sent a letter, and we met at a nearby park.

Siaza was much the worse for wear, but she also looked brighter than I'd seen her before. She'd clearly lost some weight and was still quite pale. She looked almost frail in comparison with how she was when she worked at the hotel, but she stood taller and had sharper eyes.

"I'd say you look well, but that would be a lie," I said as I joined her.

"Well, could be worse."

"Agreed, how are you?" I asked with genuine interest.

"Better than those bastards back there, or my former boss. One of your friends had them arrested." There was a small note of pleasure in her voice.

"Good, they should have known better than to do such things."

"I was their lesser to them; they could do what they wanted."

"People who treat those who serve them in such a manner don't deserve the service," I grumbled.

"Few think like that," she said, kicking her feet lightly against the small cobblestone path that ran around the bench we sat upon.

"They should. It would make the world a better place." This park was nice, and as I gave my two cents, I looked around at the trees and flowers blooming.

"What will you do now?" she inquired, moving closer.

"Go home," I said. "I've people waiting for me—family, friends, my fiancée." The words made her deflate.

"Should have known you'd have someone . . . Just my luck. You could stay here, you know. With what you've done, you'll surely have a good place amongst us."

"No doubt, but also many enemies, and if I did that, I wouldn't be who I am. A man must stick to what he believes is right, else how can he be a man? My place isn't here, and for that I am sorry."

"Well, not sure I can argue with that, which is a shame . . ."

It was around this time that I realized her clothes were newer, and much more formal than was common. Her hair was done up a little more stylishly than it had been before. It made me sigh, knowing that she wasn't the right person for me.

"And, at any rate, it wouldn't be good for you. You've only known me while on this mission, only while I was working and fighting. That's not who I am most days, and this has surely changed me in ways."

"Ha, telling me to not want a hero?"

"Perhaps it is simply the way people are, but I don't really view myself as a hero. Just a man, trying to do what he needs to do, and to help where he can."

"That's what a hero is, though with how silly you are about that, maybe you're not the best hero after all."

That got a chuckle out of me. Thinking back on it, I did somehow end up in a lot of these situations, and did, for whatever reason, always find myself stepping forward. Maybe it had something to do with how I was raised; I had been told that I needed to be responsible for those weaker than me.

"It is the duty of the strong to protect the weak, or something like that. One of the sayings from early on in our empire, or the one preceding it? Not sure exactly. Those early years were weird, but it went something like that."

"If more men lived by that mantra, I think we'd have a better world, but it seems most think it's their privilege to prey upon those weaker than them." There was a sour note in her voice.

"Then maybe you should try to change it. This land surely needs new people to rise up now, what with all the vacancies."

"I don't know anything about that though."

"Nobody does at first," I chided. "The only thing you can do to change that is to go and do it, and keep doing it until you're good at it. It's the same way with everything. Don't worry about failing, because you will—probably several times—but focus on where you failed, and where you can do better. You've been through a lot, seen a lot, and you could be a leader your people desperately need, someone from outside the system."

She laughed at me. "Well, got a suggestion on where to start?"

"I know a few people. I'll see if I can get you an interview, though don't be surprised if it isn't a particularly important position."

"That's no issue. After all, I'm not quite sure I can go back to my last job."

"I should think not, not after what happened there, though they probably owe you a last paycheck. If they give you trouble about it, let me know, and I'll see what I can do."

"Thank you, Percival, for everything." With that she leaned over, kissed my cheek, and hopped up, walking off.

That night I did indeed write her a few letters of recommendation, notes to men who might need someone. She was trustworthy, in that she had decidedly not been part of the forces causing problems, made a good poster girl, and truthfully, was quite clever. I had no doubt she'd be fine.

CHAPTER 44

✶

ATAL

I'd been pulled from the south by Councilor Chien, and frankly, I couldn't understand how he had done it, but he had wrapped mana around the two of us. It felt like being grabbed by the belly button and yanked, and suddenly, we were somewhere else.

"Welcome to Atal, and we're just in time," he said with a sweeping gesture.

We were in an office, a fairly large one, with shelves lining the walls and a massive desk covered in papers. There were also old tools—some that looked newer too— all kinds of magical items, and what looked like raw materials, many of which I couldn't identify at a glance.

"Why don't you do that all the time?" I inquired.

"Harder than it looks," he replied. "Trust me on that one. And even harder still when you're not familiar with your destination. Some random palace in some city I've only occasionally visited? Not an easy thing to do, but my own personal office that I've kept for, well, long enough? Easy as pie."

"And going across the sea like this?" I requested, hopefully.

"Not a chance. Too far for me, and I don't know that area well enough, at any rate."

"Wait, can all wizards do this?" I asked, thinking about the possibilities.

"Masters can, if they try hard enough, and practice hard enough, and are just this side of genius. Never seen a human do it, between you and me, but it wouldn't surprise me if there have been one or two who could." I could see him looking at a watch and nodding sagely, but he didn't elaborate.

With a slight bristling, I narrowed my eyes. "Seriously, didn't we just go after people who thought themselves better?"

"I have the advantage of time. If I had the short life span of your people, I wouldn't have managed it, because I'm not the brightest of my kind, Percival. It took me over three hundred years just to manage my first. Though, at this point, I am empirically stronger than any living human . . . wizard."

"Do I want to ask?" I said, the qualification pinging something.

"No." His tone was clear, even if it still sounded like he was half joking.

"It's hard to get a read on you."

"That's the point, kid. See, I'm the problem, the joker, the old man who acts a fool. It puts people at ease, let's them relax, let's me see the truth. Been this way since I was a child. Isn't that a fun thought—me, a child. It helps to show what's really behind the lies, behind the little falsehoods we tell even ourselves. You get to watch how people respond, how they really act when they aren't afraid of you."

"And your thoughts on me?"

"You've acquitted yourself well. You're still a kid, but you clearly care, even for those lesser than yourself. That girl. You didn't need to save her, didn't need to give her those recommendations either." Something on my face must have shown. "Yes, I knew about that too. Why'd you do it?"

"In a few ways, she reminds me of my sister, and it was the right thing to do," I told him, meeting his eyes.

"That's the truth. She reminds you of someone you care about, indeed. I think that's most of it. It was also the right thing to do, and you seem the kind to want to do what you think is right."

"Of course . . ."

"Be careful. Sometimes the thing we're so sure is right is nothing but harmful. It's a hard lesson to learn, and too many of us don't learn it soon enough. Think, consider, and understand everything before you act, if you must act, then act decisively and without malice."

I took a seat in a chair before the main desk, which the councilor decided to tidy up a little before settling in.

"Giving me life advice at this point? Well, I suppose you've given me some already."

"I've been trying, and trying is important."

"Why though?"

He took his seat at his desk and considered for a few moments, tapping his chin and leaning back. "Your grandfather is from the north of this continent. Man, I miss the giant trees. His family has lived there for seven generations. Did you know that?"

"I knew they were from there, and pretty well off, before he got driven out, at least."

"Extremely well off. Most of his family, to this day, has a much higher than average level of elven blood, and a much higher than average propensity for magic. Now this is a secret not many know, but the stronger you get with magic, the more your children inherit. Weird, huh? No idea why, but it's true."

"Interesting, but what does that have to do with anything? And why do you know so much about . . . Oh, come now, don't tell me . . ."

"A dalliance some eight hundred years ago. Lovely girl, but our daughter moved, and your line mixed with humans more often than not. I mean that quite literally. Some of your distant cousins may live to be many hundreds of years old—a good age."

"So you're my many-times-over great grandfather, then, and you feel responsible?"

"Probably, assuming nobody had an affair, which is a bit of a half and half, at best, but you're probably descended from me, regardless. I've had a lot of kids over the years, and those bloodlines have spread like wildfire. I try to keep up with the bloodlines, but honestly, it's becoming a bit of a chore."

"You're an absolute menace, aren't you?"

"Granted, but better to have a menace on your side than against you, isn't it? Now, let's get you home!"

He turned and moved for the door, and I followed suit. We appeared to be in some sort of massive compound, with a larger city visible out the windows, much of it behind a wall. The halls were made of stone, clean and wide. They felt old somehow, but I couldn't really put my finger on why. There were a few elves, men and women, moving about doing various tasks, some with papers, a few cleaning, whom the councilor nodded to.

"Always know the cleaners. Another tidbit of advice for you, kid. Cleaners can get things done."

"Noted. The goblins? Greta and her son, are they all right?" He seemed in a hurry, taking long strides.

"Fine, perfectly fine. We've got a warship near their island, and she's trying to rebuild. We've been doing some reclamation on it, but that place is going to be a mess for at least a generation, well, a human generation."

"We'll have to get their people who are back in our lands sorted," I said. "Some might want to settle there . . ."

"Sounds like a plan, though, your government will probably be involved with that."

"Assuredly," I answered with a sigh.

Through twisting halls, we eventually found ourselves outside, in a large courtyard. People didn't stare, but they didn't ignore us either, seeming used to the white-haired man I walked beside. He led me over to a building that made my skin itch. Magic was palpable around it, glowing runes on every surface, every wall humming with power contained in it.

"What's this?"

"A portal building. It's how you're getting home." We entered through the front, doors opening for us automatically.

"Aren't those scheduled?" I asked. That much was common knowledge. We moved deeper in, past checkpoint after checkpoint, and soon we found ourselves in a small room, surrounded on all sides by what were clearly weapon emplacements. Already, there was a glowing blue aperture inside a circular gate.

"Sure are," he answered cheerily, "and we're just in time for this next one. Now, I'd love to stick around and chat, but you've got an appointment, and these windows are short, and mostly for diplomats, so, any final questions?"

"Wait, did you schedule this? How, how did you even know how long I was going to chat with you?"

"Give it long enough and you get a feel for how long conversations take. Now, off you go!" I wasn't really near the portal, but I was still lifted and thrown.

"Wait! What are you doing?!" I yelled as I flew toward it which, in retrospect, seemed a poor choice of a final question.

"Sending you home kid. Bye!"

I tried to keep yelling, but there wasn't time for anything much before I plunged face first into the gateway.

CHAPTER 45

✶

ACADEMY

"You son of a bitch!" I screamed as I tumbled out the other side of the portal, end over end, hard enough to send me sprawling, but not quite hard enough to actually hurt.

"Oh, look, another one," I heard from somewhere behind me. "You owe me lunch."

By the time I popped up and turned, the portal had closed, leaving an empty aperture behind me. Incensed, I turned to where the voice had come from. There were two human men sitting at a small control station.

"Restart it," I commanded, anger in my voice.

"No, sir, I'm afraid that would be unsafe. We're unable to open portals, except at designated times or in a genuine emergency. You know this. I can see you know this, and you being angry isn't an emergency."

I nearly snapped at him again, but thought better of it. It would be like screaming at a TSA agent—poorly advised and likely to get you on the no-fly list. I could feel the pulsing of a vein in my head, though, and a small twitch in my eye.

"Very well," I said through gritted teeth. "Where exactly am I?"

"The Royal Magic Academy."

"Which one?" I asked for clarification. There were several magical academies, and at least three had that name. There was one in the capital, one in the south, and one on the main campus in the far north. Many had other names, as well, but all fell under this general umbrella.

"The primary campus. I do hate to be a stickler for protocol"—Everyone with a brain knew that was a lie—"but I don't suppose you have your travel documents?"

"You've seen people thrown through before. Did they have theirs?" It was clear I didn't, because someone hadn't thought to issue me any new ones. Most of my things were gone, save what I had on me.

"Certainly not."

"Then what do you expect?" I asked.

"We'll need to confirm your identity somehow. Perhaps you have someone we could contact?"

"Wait, the main northern campus?"

"Yes."

"Please ask for a student named Rowenna. School should be in session now," I informed him.

"A sister or cousin, then?"

"Fiancée."

"Oh, of course. That will do perfectly well. Please fill out these forms." He passed over a stack of paperwork that I started on while his coworker leaned over to whisper.

"See, this one didn't explode. Now you owe me lunch." At those words, the twitch came back, with a vengeance.

"Does he do this often?" I asked as I continued to work through the forms.

"Basically every time we have an incoming scheduled from that area, and before you ask, scheduling a return trip is probably not worth the time."

"You think someone would complain?"

"I'm quite sure they do, sir. However, I'm to understand that some of the older elves get *eccentric* with age."

"That's one way of putting it, yes. A right pain in the backside is another way of putting it. Then again, if nobody opposes you . . . How much do you know about the person who handles the other side of that gate?"

"Basically nothing, and I'm not supposed to, beyond the fact that it is an old elf. Even the old headmistress only used that gate once every few years." He thought for a moment. "Though, she herself would have easily been described as eccentric too—brilliant pillar of our country, but eccentric."

"People probably say that I am too . . ." I mumbled, finishing up the last of the forms and handing them over. There was a lot that wasn't on there, but they didn't ask, and I wasn't going to say.

It was only minutes later that a familiar face came through the door on the far end of the hall at speed. She didn't run, but her normally slow, deliberate walk was sped up as much as it could be without compromising her posture. Training for proper behavior was deeply engrained, after all. Though, I could hear her heels clicking on the stone and was surprised she was managing the speed she was. Perhaps magic was involved somewhere in the movement.

"What in the world are you doing here?! Not that I mind; it's just unexpected. I was waiting for letters to reach us first and expected you on a boat. I know that it takes time, but coming through a portal . . . Was there even a portal you could access in Elazia? If there was, why in the world did you leave by boat in the first place. That seems silly! Are you all right, Percival? You look dreadful!" It all came out as one breath, and I waited for her to finish.

"I've missed you, too, Rowenna, and it's a long story. Sadly, I can't share most of it, but things are well, and will improve, I think."

"I hate to interrupt . . ." Really, these men did like to lie.

"Yes, yes, he's Percival Shadestone. I can confirm, yes. Come now, dear, let's talk." She was more excited than I'd probably ever seen her and had me by the hand pulling before I knew what was happening.

I didn't resist, happy to have a reason to get away from the men who really liked their paperwork and their bets more than anything else. So, she led me, out and away, toward the school proper. I wasn't a student here, but she didn't seem to care, and I assumed she knew the rules better than I. It wasn't like I could just hop a portal home anyway. Those were all on strict timetables.

"You've missed so very much. Your sister has been doing magnificently, by the way, for someone so new to this. Few issues here and there, but nothing we can't smooth out. Oh, and her friend really is the hit of the year—polite, well-spoken, and genuinely civilized. Though, there's more problems where that's concerned. A lot of people are still quite sore about the goblins and their attack, but perhaps that can be smoothed over in time."

"I doubt that deeply, Rowenna, but we can do what we can. People won't forgive lost homes and family members, but they might put the blame in the right place instead, or at least most of it. Has there been violence?"

"Some, truthfully, but not as much as one might fear. Come, we can talk about it while I show you around." She was clearly taking me to a main courtyard, one surrounded by buildings and full of students.

"Is this a tour or a chance for you to show me off to your school friends?" I inquired with a smile.

"Both, of course. So do try to behave."

CHAPTER 46

✶

RETURNING HOME: PART ONE

For a full afternoon, and part of the evening, I was paraded around Rowenna's school like a show dog. She took me to her friends, and then to several groups of students who I gathered were her enemies. She basically told them how cool I was, how strong and brave, and even said, "Isn't he nice? He just got back from the elven continent. Do you know anyone who's been?" It was a bit tiring, and not something that could go on forever.

At some point, someone had arranged lodging for me, but only for the night. This facility was still primarily a school. It just had a travel hub attached, and I wasn't a student here. That alone made my presence dubious. I did, at least, get the chance to prepare a few letters for my family.

"Do you happen to know where my mother has gone?" I asked Rowenna. "Things were still a bit up in the air when I left."

"Retired to the country estate for a period of mourning. Though, she has called for the city home to be rebuilt, ostensibly for you. Your sister is staying at your paternal grandparents' place in Exion, and you do need to see both of them as soon as possible."

"Is something wrong?" I asked, confused about the last thing she said.

"Your mother took everything poorly. I think her period of mourning is much about that as well. She's a strong woman, but knowing you're well will give her a great deal of peace. We correspond frequently."

"You correspond with everyone frequently," I pointed out.

"Of course, but the letters get to her slowly. They really should put a portal closer to that place."

"A common complaint. I don't suppose you can give me a quick rundown of what's happening with my other family members?"

"Kaylee is a doll, but having a bit of trouble adjusting; nothing one wouldn't expect. However, things aren't going as smoothly with the goblins. Everyone wants them out, and while it's plain to see that there are factions, well . . ."

"Plenty of people don't care."

"Yes, quite."

"I saw their island. It's not good, but they can rebuild there."

"Are their cousins so bad?"

"Their cousins were exterminated by a terrible faction of elves." That comment got Rowenna to freeze for a full minute, eyes wide. She sat upon the bed I was borrowing, taken fully aback. "And the ones who did it are dead, too, for what they did. The whole thing was an ugly affair. It will probably be in the papers in a couple months, knowing how things travel between the continents."

"Heavens, what happened?"

"I can't tell you more than I have, I'm afraid," I explained shaking my head. "Secrets and all."

She didn't pry. She wanted to; that much was clear on her face, but she respected my decision. That was worth a lot, truly a lot. Rowenna may have loved her gossip, but she knew when state secrets were involved it was best to let it lie.

"Well, what can you tell me?" she asked.

"Tomorrow morning, over breakfast," I said with a smile.

"Deal."

Breakfast was an art form in this nation. It made for a very good date, and one that had fallen in and out of style a few times over the years. The next morning, I told Rowenna what I could—the plants and flowers, the architecture, the language. I told her that many elves seemed a bit too proud of themselves, which got a laugh and a small pull at my own slightly pointed ears.

Then, I bid her farewell with a kiss on the cheek and headed to the portal. I slipped a letter to a courier service to see that my mother at least knew I was well and on my way back, even if it would be some time yet before I was home.

As I stepped back into the open air of Exion, I took a deep breath, not really thinking, then I nearly retched. The city still stank to high heaven; it always had. I'd just gotten used to the stench of sewage and horse manure over the years. Time away had taken that inoculation from me, and I'd not even considered it.

My first, and primary, stop was the city home of my paternal grandfather, Baron Shadestone. He was a man with more power politically and economically than anyone else in the family, and personally potent to boot. Sadly, the announcement of my arrival came only a few minutes before I did.

A hired coach took me, weaving through the old streets, and in directions I found a bit odd. Then it hit me as a sight line cleared, and I could see where my old home had been. Construction. A whole block had been effectively leveled, and the area around it ripped up too. Perhaps survivable, perhaps not. Men worked around the site where my father had died, masons and carpenters rebuilding, lines for property being taken, streets repaved and pipes reset. It hurt to watch, but the strike had likely saved much of the city by taking out such a large part of the enemy forces.

Yet, the city remained. It was nearly normal: the sound of the horses' hooves audible on the ancient cobbles, the people going to the market and chatting, children playing, men working, women moving to and fro on errands—some of the women were housewives, some had jobs. Exion lived; it was hurt, injured, but alive.

As the wheels rolled to a stop, I saw the butler rushing out. The poor man looked stressed.

"Lord Percival," he said, as the footmen followed in his wake, just short of running as that would be improper. "My apologies for the lack of welcome, sir. We weren't expecting—"

"At ease," I said. "There was no way you could have known. Things have moved fast. Tell me, is my grandfather home?"

"I'm afraid he's at the duke's residence. Some business . . ." he began and trailed off with my knowing nod. "The baroness is here though. I understand she's sent the cooks into battle to prepare dinner tonight."

That brought a genuine laugh, something welcome these days. "Let's not keep her waiting a moment longer, then, shall we?" I suggested, but she met us before we even entered, hugging me at the threshold.

"Come inside, come inside," she bade me, a hand taking my arm. "You gave me a shock with that letter of yours."

"It's good to see you too," I told her, stepping alongside her. Really, I had missed too much.

CHAPTER 47

✶

RETURNING HOME: PART TWO

Grandmother was doting, but before too long, and before too many sweets had been shoved in front of me, I had to ask.

"Kaylee?"

"Out at a lovely little charity event she's aiding. Kind girl, bless her. Wouldn't have thought I'd be raising another child at my age, but here we are."

"No trouble?" I prodded.

"Nothing more than growing pains. Her mother has a small place not too far from here. We got her a job, something low key, out of the public eye. That's better for everyone, sad for her, but . . . well, it's best not to dwell too long on it. She's fine, and will be."

I let it drop, knowing there was little to be done beyond that. I didn't hate the woman. She'd all but raised me, but at the same time, I understood that, for Kaylee to grow, her mother would need to stay out of the public eye. It was brutal, it was hard, but it was the way things were in this society, and I could do little about it.

"And you, where's your luggage?" Grandmother asked. "I didn't see them bring anything in."

"Ah, it was misplaced," I admitted.

"On an official mission for the state? You should ask them to reimburse you. It's the least those elves could do."

"I think they did enough, for all of us," I retorted calmly. I could probably get clothes reimbursed, but more than likely, there would be some joke sent along with it that I really just didn't want to deal with.

"We'll see to it tomorrow, then. You can't go home with only one pair of trousers. It's unseemly." I laughed at her. She was not as uptight as my grandma, but still just the person for this job.

My grandfather got home not too long afterward, looking tired, but perking up brightly when he saw me.

"Percival! Oh, my boy, come here. I didn't know you were back yet. When did you arrive?"

"Just a few hours ago," I said through the massive bear hug he gave me. He wasn't a physical magic user like I was, but he was still a giant of a man, well built.

"Come then, we've much to discuss. Let us retire to my reading room. I've gotten a bit of whiskey in you can help me appraise." I was a bit young for drinking, but I had before, and it wasn't like there was an age restriction.

"Before dinner?" Grandmother asked, an eyebrow raised.

"Oh, he's a man. He can take a bit of the old fire and still be himself," Grandfather Shadestone huffed, leading me away.

"Don't worry, Grandmother, I won't drink too much."

My grandfather knew well enough that there wasn't much I could tell him. I'd have to compose a report for the king and the duke later, and Grandfather might get read in on that, but it wasn't either of our calls. There was something I could say though.

"Those responsible for Auntie Penumbra's premature death have been dealt with, and with prejudice. We have little to fear in the coming years with the elven nations, so far as I know, and the goblins will have a home soon. The island they were living on was rendered dead and is currently being replanted."

"The whole island?!" he asked, shocked.

"Looked like a mix of artillery, heavy magic, and priests destroying anything they found; bare rock," I clarified.

"Heavens," he murmured, sipping on his whiskey. "You should be the one to tell miss Sasha. You've had dealings with her before, and your sister would be poorly suited for this. Better to come from a . . . well, maybe not friend, but ally, at least."

Kaylee got home while the two of us were talking, not about anything in particular, just life in general. He had three drinks to my one, but didn't look like it affected him in the slightest. He gave me advice on women and how to run a home, and he mused a lot.

"You know, when you were a boy, you defended Kaylee, and I asked you to keep making me as proud as I was of you that day."

"I remember," I told him, "and I've certainly tried."

"You've more than succeeded, son. Ah, enough of this. If we take too much longer, your grandmother might come up here to find us."

"She's stopping Kaylee from doing just that," I said, laughing, tapping my ears. I'd heard enough of their conversation to know who was keeping things here private. It wasn't appropriate for her to come and interrupt men speaking over drinks, after all. We might even have been smoking (we weren't), and propriety was very important.

"An even better reason!" He laughed, and together we headed to see them.

Dinner that night was a long affair, slightly less formal than was typical. Celebratory. Kaylee was well, doing charity work as she practiced her magic. That was good and would help her overall. It was a very social thing a lot of young women did. Among nobles there was an undercurrent of responsibility, in theory, if not in truth, for those below them, and this was seen as young women fulfilling that responsibility.

Nor was there a lack of need for her work. She told me how they helped many people displaced by the fighting. Lots of homes had been damaged or destroyed, and while they were being rebuilt slowly, it wasn't like the people who'd lived there—the servants or residents—were doing great.

We talked and ate, then went to the sitting room and talked some more, well into the night. It was good, and I got to actually treat Kaylee as my sister, something I'd done little of while I was training for my mission, and hardly at all in the many years prior.

"Goodnight, Percival," she said, not even stumbling while addressing me as she retired to her room.

"Goodnight, Kaylee," I responded in kind.

CHAPTER 48

✶

RETURNING HOME: PART THREE

I met Sasha the next morning, in the duke's palace. I'd needed to come here to deliver my reports anyway. As I entered the room she was practically bouncing with anticipation.

Her demeanor changed as I explained what I'd found. I assured her that her sister was well the last I saw her, and that I'd heard the same recently. The child was fine too. The goblins on the island, however . . . She didn't know how to take it. I saw her go through a whole stream of emotions as I spoke, and I reinforced my body against magic. She was still powerful, and I wouldn't want to come to feel what she could do.

"Why?" she asked at the end, eyes looking off to the west.

"Stories, from my understanding. Written by a man who hadn't known your kind, or even that your kind actually existed. They were just stories, scary tales of monsters that looked like little green men. In them, they were truly terrible and dangerous. The people who had read the stories believed them to be real, believed them to be evidence, and rather than risk it . . . they were vicious and stupid."

"They killed my people over bedtime stories," she said, hollow. "You said the ones who did it were held responsible. Tell me, did they suffer?"

"Yes, but Sasha, don't go down the road of hate. It's too easy to hate, and too easy to lose yourself to it. They suffered because they fought, but justice doesn't require suffering, not always."

"You're right, but I still find I prefer if those who would act in such ways would serve as an example."

"Agreed, and you have allies now too. Some of the elves are interested in helping as much as they can to repair the damage that was done. Your people have a home, one where you can build and become great."

"We'll need rules, laws, but it'll be good to have somewhere to call home. Frankly, I think your people are getting a bit tired of us being here."

"I've heard, but obviously, I've been away."

"Ha, that's one way of putting it. At least you saw to justice. We won't forget that, Percival—you or the elves that are helping. I don't suppose you can give me their names?"

"You'll meet them in time, and frankly, I'm not sure that I can say. They are allies, though, from a place called Atal."

"Good, I'll remember." She left after that.

The duke read my report once, said nothing, and had sent me straight to the portal in the capital. It took almost an hour for His Majesty to see me himself, which was, frankly, insane, since I'd been expecting to wait days to get an audience with a literal sovereign. Apparently, being a key part in collapsing the government of an oppositional nation got you sent up in line.

The room we met in wasn't some giant hall, but a large office-like arrangement, almost like a board room, if not for the heavy, black curtains and the small but literal throne the man at the head of the table sat on. There were even a few servants handing out drinks to the various advisors and leaders—cold water and juice.

"There are two mentioned in your report, the ambassador and another. Who was the other?" he asked, eyebrows furrowed.

"Might I ask that you clear the room of everyone possible?" I requested.

With a wave it was done. The servers headed for the door. Half of the advisors too. Five men were left, all military, or spy types. They were older, and one guard, a man who had stood near the king but had not spoken during the meeting.

"His Majesty decided to intervene personally," I said, not giving a name.

"His Majesty was here," one of the generals replied, gesturing toward the king and narrowing his eyes at me. "He sent you."

"Not *our* king, nor a *human* king."

"Oh . . . OH," the head of the nation's spy network said, leaning back.

"Can someone fill me in?" the king asked.

"The elves only ever had one king," I told him. I really didn't want to say his name, just in case. "And I suspect he is the one our ambassador calls 'boss.'"

The string of obscenities loosed by my nation's ruler was, frankly, impressive. I'd never heard him curse once in our few interactions, but if I ever needed to do so with aplomb, he'd given me ample lessons from which to learn in those few moments.

"Did my aunt know?" he finally roared.

"I got the feeling they were good friends. It's part of the reason he was interested in who attacked her," I said. "So I must presume, yes."

"That old wrinkled hag! She never told me a lick of that!"

"To be fair, Your Majesty, it was probably a good decision, one we should all emulate . . ." the spymaster bravely said.

"Don't you start with me too!" He took a few breaths, and while I thought he was going to start up with the colorful language again, he didn't. He calmed. "No word of this leaves this room. Elven ancients are queer and dangerous creatures on the best of days, and we *certainly* do not want their secrets spilled by our lips." There were nods and murmurs of agreement on all sides. I, for one, wanted nothing more to do with it.

With that I was released, with warnings of course. The fastest public way for me to get to the country house was actually through Exion. For how silly that was, and while access to the military portal network might have been granted had I asked, I didn't.

Instead, I returned to the city where I'd lived so long, and got on a boat. It was a proper end to things, returning to the place I'd been born, if only for a while, via the same route I'd first traveled there. Sure, it took days, but I spent them in meditation, relaxing, enjoying a bit of conversation with other men on board. It was nostalgic, enjoyable.

The journey took me from the long boat ride across the cold northern seas, then to a shorter one through fields of golden grain via train and, finally, to a carriage rolling down old roads through gentle hills. I was far from the bustling city and well out into the country, to a proud old manor house I knew like my own hand.

My mother, having heard word of my return, came out to greet me. She was dressed in dark colors, and though her face was cracked with a sadness she'd had since father's death, there was a smile too.

"I'm home," I told her, walking across the short path to the door.

"Welcome back, son," she replied, reaching out to pull me inside after so long away.

EPILOGUE

✶

Three Years Later

"I don't know why you're so insistent on running this on volatiles of all things, my boy. There are better ways to do it," Grandpa Darksky said as he leaned over the engine.

In the last few years, his age was starting to show. He still looked like a man far, far younger than he was, but age comes for us all. Well, most of us.

"Because doing it with magic is already being done. The work is more interesting, and it allows people without access to mana to do it themselves," I said, sleeves rolled up as I made adjustments. "We could even use these in planes."

"Please don't joke, Percival. Those, at least, should remain attached to reason." I laughed, but he didn't.

I flipped a switch, and man, the thing was loud, roaring as it started up, turning to life as it consumed fuel and spat smoke and energy out in response. It wasn't anything complicated, basically a two-stroke engine.

"Have to do something about the smell," I said, coughing a bit.

"I quite agree," he replied, as he cast a spell to make the air flow out of our little outdoor workshop.

"Works well enough, though, if a bit slow."

"Please tell me you're not planning to have this thing anywhere near your wedding," Grandpa said with a harsh look.

"What? No! Nothing of the sort. Rowenna would skin me alive." Even as I said it, though, I pictured it: a few metal cups, a small sign with JUST MARRIED on the back . . . No, no, it wouldn't make sense to anyone, and she would be livid. It would be funny though.

"Rightly so!" we said in unison, having gotten used to each other enough to have the good sense to say certain things in chorus. We laughed.

"Ready for it?" he asked as I wiped the oil from my hands.

"Honestly? No, not at all."

"Good answer," he said. "Probably means you're as ready as you will be. Though, between us, I think it wiser to stay out here a bit longer. The women are fussing in there, and I want no part of it."

Fussing had been going on for days—weeks even—and would almost certainly continue ad infinitum, should the time be given for it. My family, hers, friends, some people we didn't know, all piled into the small home we had rebuilt in Exion.

Rowenna had insisted we have the ceremony there, during the Season, so everyone could make it, and I'd always been rather bad at not giving her what she wanted. So, even her many friends from school were coming by. A few of mine were too. Her brother was, by far, the most annoying of them. He kept wanting to spar with me.

Neither Sasha nor Greta would be making an appearance, as they had an island with a skyrocketing population to rule, and had growing families of their own. They did send their well wishes, which was for the best. Goblins were still causing problems in the area around Exion, and showing no signs of stopping, and it was a whole thing these days.

But those were worries for another time. There was a form of peace, a family who loved me, and a lot of work to do. I wanted us to rise to a level of technology the elves thought they had; and while I couldn't build all of it, perhaps I could turn over the engine of progress just a bit, give it just a little of a kickstart. That was enough for me, one more cog in the whole, one more piece in the growth of the world, into what would hopefully be a better one than I'd known before.

ABOUT THE AUTHOR

Wandering Agent is the North Carolina–based author of the Melody of Mana series as well as other fantasy and isekai stories.

www.ingramcontent.com/pod-product-compliance
Lightning Source LLC
LaVergne TN
LVHW091302150826
845673LV00006B/1514

* 9 7 9 8 8 9 5 3 9 8 7 7 7 *